CHASING THE DUKE

TRACY SUMNER

CHASING THE DUKE

Copyright © 2020 by Tracy Sumner

Print ISBN: 979-8689471617

All rights reserved.

No part of this book may be reproduced in any form or by any electronic or mechanical means, including information storage and retrieval systems, without written permission from the author, except for the use of brief quotations in a book review.

Edited by: Casey Harris-Parks

ACKNOWLEDGMENTS

Huge shout-out to my devoted, wonderful Street Team! Thank you for your support, encouragement and friendship. I've enjoyed our discussions about books and life and hope for many more!

ALSO BY TRACY SUMNER

Garrett Brothers Series

Tides of Love

Tides of Passion

Tides of Desire: A Christmas Romance

Southern Heat Series

To Seduce a Rogue

To Desire a Scoundrel: A Christmas Seduction

League of Lords Series

The Lady is Trouble

The Rake is Taken

The Duke is Wicked (*coming 2021*)

Multi-Author Series

Tempting the Scoundrel

Multi-Author Anthologies

A Scandalous Christmas

Chasing the Duke: Seventh Day of Christmas

CHAPTER 1

Where childhood adversaries argue over a swan.

Longleat Manor, North Yorkshire, England
The Seventh Day of Christmas, 1815

She wasn't chasing a duke ever again.
 Never, ever, *ever*.

Camille Bellington yanked a dangling thread from her sleeve and blew a breath that anyone who heard it would excuse as refined from her lips.

She couldn't believe he'd been invited.

She knew precisely *why* he'd been invited.

Camille sent a penetrating stare down the enormous table dominating her aunt's formal dining room, her lips pressed hard enough to crack. Lady Isabel Fontaine snickered at something the Earl of Edelman said, refusing to catch her niece's eye when Camille's gaze must have scorched. Her aunt loved nothing more than a dash of fun at someone else's expense.

"You're wasting those smoldering looks on the hardest head in England, Princess. Lady Fontaine couldn't care less about your high dander. She wants a spot of entertainment, and we're it."

Surprised by his astuteness, Camille glanced at Tristan Tierney, the fifth Duke of Mercer, for the first time all evening. Through a trembling candlelit glimmer, the clack of crystal and silverware a dull chime in her ear, his undeniable, bombastic magnificence flowed through her to lodge quite faithfully in her belly, an unwelcome return. Dressed head to toe in black except for his loosely-tied cravat and pressed linen shirt, eyes glowing, teeth flashing, dark hair mussed just so, he presented a dazzling ducal puzzle every woman in the *ton* longed to solve.

More the fool, she found she couldn't look away.

Even though she loathed him.

Truly. Like a toothache, a hangnail, a shallow cut on the tip of one's finger that took forever to heal.

Her wound had taken *years* to heal.

As Tristan bestowed his absolute attention on her for the first time in memory, her mind went hazy. Usually, she was an unseen annoyance—his best friend's much younger sister—but curiously his unblinking gaze fastened her to her chair like an insect caught in amber.

He'd always been handsome, but now it was worse. Time had carved grooves alongside his mouth, hardened his jaw, broadened his shoulders.

Made a man from a boy.

The chattering throng her aunt had invited to a rousing Christmastide dinner didn't understand the change, but she did. There were no obvious scars from the Battle of Waterloo, and he'd made light of requests for heroic narratives, but

Tristan's eyes, as green as a bearberry leaf, held a thousand teasing secrets that attracted and repelled in turn.

A blatant appeal should one be set on unlocking a gorgeous mystery, which Camille was not.

And hadn't been for years.

Countess Milburn, seated to his right, gave a breathy sigh and tapped her butter knife on his wrist, which would have been scandalous had she not been thirty years his senior and generally regarded as the grande dame of England. "Mercer, darling, you were going to tell us about your plans for your ancestral estate now that your father has passed on, may he rest in peace."

Tristan's smile was a dreamy display of graciousness, believable for anyone who hadn't assiduously studied it. "Was I?" he murmured, his gaze sliding away and allowing Camille to bring a frankincense-and-roasted-goose breath into her lungs. "I believe I was about to ask Lady Bellington to recount the time she tussled with a swan in the Serpentine. A perfect topic for the season. And apropos. Aren't they the symbol for the seventh day of Christmas?"

The choice of subject, and the wry amusement in his voice, sent a bolt of fury through Camille. She glanced around the table, realizing the Duke of Mercer had balanced the entire focus of the room atop her head like an ill-fitting bonnet. Bringing her glass to her lips, she took a revitalizing sip of wine before speaking. "That's a rumor. And an ancient one."

He laughed around a bite of goose, chewed slowly, smiled wickedly, before lifting his gaze and snaring hers again. Pinned right to her chair, indeed. "Don't go down that path. I saw the poor beast after the battle if you recall."

"You bring this up," she whispered, "to divert attention from yourself."

"An effective strategy," he volleyed, "and I'm nothing if

not a well-trained soldier. What's surprising to me is that you're still upset about an event that happened years ago." He shrugged a broad shoulder and shared a slice of his devastating charm with the room's inhabitants as if to say, *petty of her, am I right?*

"It was partially your fault. You and Edward." Her brother had hooted when she fell into the pond as if he'd never seen such a thing. Who tried to pet a swan, after all? Then he'd sighed and begun the process of dragging her out, a bold rescue of his reckless sister from the grasp of an enraged fowl.

Tristan tipped his glass toward her with an elegant turn of his wrist. "You're the one who said swans were nice. We tried to tell you they're bloody nasty, not to touch. I don't even know why we brought you along. Your governess begged us to, I suspect."

"You arrogant cur," she said for his ears alone.

"You brash hoyden," he returned for hers, his ghost of a smile proving he was *enjoying* this.

"Children, children, let's not argue," Lady Fontaine admonished from her spot at the head of the table. The jewels circling her wrist, paste because they'd had to sell the real ones to pay the bills, created a merry chime as she waved her hand in the air, a magician without a wand. "Family friends, it's all in good fun," she added, a vapid explanation Camille guessed no one believed.

Though Tristan had often circled her orbit during her childhood, they'd never been friends. But her aunt had always treated Tristan like family, provided shelter and encouragement when he and his father got into the raging battles that later drove an heir to a dukedom to join Wellington's army and ride away to Belgium.

Not once looking back to see who he'd left behind.

"Obviously more enemies than friends," Countess Milburn tittered.

Tristan blinked and tilted his head as if the idea hadn't occurred to him. When she'd thought it a thousand times herself. "Who says we're enemies," he murmured and gave Camille a look that said something her mind didn't understand but her body, *oh*, the wash of heat centering in her belly and moving into a neat tuck between her thighs…

Viscount Ridley slapped his glass to the table, spraying wine across starched linen and china. "Mercer, hold up, you're embarrassing my intended. I suppose you must be reminded of courteous behavior now that you're off the battlefield."

Tristan halted, his glass suspended halfway to his lips. His eyes when they met hers were flat, a verdict she wasn't sure how to interpret. "That's not embarrassment on Lady Bellington's face, Ridley, it's anger." He finished his motion, polished off his wine, looking down his aristocratic nose at the man she'd only yesterday accepted a proposal from. "You'd better learn to recognize the difference, or you're in for a grueling matrimonial haul."

"As if I'd take your—"

"I should add, I think it best you don't mention a battlefield to someone recently removed." Tristan peered into his glass as if wishing more wine would appear. "We fighting men tend to get testy about such matters, lack of courteous behavior as you so kindly mentioned."

Her aunt jumped into the fray, willing to roll the dice for fun but not with malicious intent. And dipping a toe into the disaster of a pond that was the Battle of Waterloo was going too far, even for her. "Aren't the floral arrangements adorning the room gorgeous? The mix of evergreens, holly, and English fir a scrumptious holiday presence? The cinnamon sticks interspersed throughout a brilliant touch. I wanted to bring the forest inside the manor, incorporating the fragrances of winter and Christmas, with as much color as the season could provide. Out of season, hothouse varieties being too steep for my purse, you see."

"Lovely, Lady Fontaine, just lovely." Countess Milburn touched a pine needle with her gloved finger. "You can evaluate the decorations for my annual winter ball in two days if you enjoy that sort of thing. I know you'll be in attendance. I was exceptionally disappointed with last year's preparations. And to think, I've used Germaine and Sons for years."

Her aunt laughed and patted her ample chest, eyes sparkling in a way Camille had come to fear over the years, hard little sapphires glowing in the candlelight. "Oh, dear me, I'm as untalented as one can be with floral arrangements and the like. Every shrub I plant dies a quick death, pathetic things. My gardener cannot even bring them back once I step in."

Giving her head a firm shake, Camille sent another pleading look down the table. *Not here, not now.*

But when had Isabel Fontaine ever followed any whim but her own?

"My niece created each flowery composition you see in this mausoleum of a house. Longleat could not survive without her. Camille has been interested in plants, cuttings, and such since she was in leading strings. It's her special talent when most women in the *ton* aren't allowed one. An interest of their own *and* the freedom to explore it. But with her parent's demise when she was five, I was left to manage her upbringing in my way. Spinster aunts are a strange lot, aren't we?" Lady Fontaine patted her lips with her napkin and pretended to ignore the horrified looks being once again aimed in Camille's direction. "Her conservatory is nothing short of a museum dedicated to the study of botany. Fascinating aside from the spider webs and teeny-tiny insects and smell of decaying organisms. My library is filled with gardening texts, too, floor to ceiling. The girl always has her nose stuck in one. A book that is. Or a hand buried wrist-deep in dirt. She even corresponds with a botanical group in London. A group of *men*. A riveting hobby, isn't that right, my dear?"

Camille took a slow sip of wine and closed her eyes. Counted to five as she considered why her aunt raised this topic when she knew Viscount Ridley would be horrified. Of course, the plan had been to tell him. At some point. When it was too late for him to back out and ruin her design to enter into a loveless marriage to save Longleat Manor from creditors. "It's a business," she finally muttered after a charged silence, as the gathering processed the idea of the daughter of a marquess having a special *talent*. A *business*. Reading biological texts and meeting with men, if only by letter. It sounded shocking, even to her, when listed out like that.

"How industrious," Countess Milburn murmured in a tone stating it was anything but.

Viscount Ridley smoothed his hand—a rather handsome hand, slim fingers and neat, clipped nails—down his crimson waistcoat. Over the slight, very *manageable*, bulge that was his belly. "Well, this endeavor will end with our marriage. It's no wonder you've been around for a season or two longer than anyone with your grace and undeniable beauty should have, Lady Camille. No viscountess has a hobby such as this. Practically sounds, dear God, *academic*."

Awareness fluttered through her like someone had trailed a finger along her skin. Camille blinked to find the Duke of Mercer's piercing gaze fixed on her. He made no effort, none at all, to hide the challenge coloring his emerald eyes almost black.

Tell them, his look said, *go on*.

Oh, that rebellious encouragement had nearly led to a

swan's death, as he'd told the entire gathering, thank you very much. She'd come close to drowning in the Serpentine. *And* embarrassed herself for life in front of the man she'd loved since her first memory of him.

Glancing at the slice of nougat almond cake on her plate, Camille tapped the thistle branch she'd wrapped in gold ribbon and placed by each place setting, completely giving up the ghost. "I retained thirty accounts from the florist in Helmsley when he retired last year. In actuality, I make a tidy sum, which has kept Longleat afloat, if I may be so crass as to admit it. Celtic sprays, love knots, bridal bouquets, consulting on gardens in distress and the like keep me—"

"You make *money?*" Viscount Ridley clutched his chest as if his heart had stopped with the news.

"For aiding gardens in distress," Tristan added in a deafening voice as if the viscount was hard of hearing. "Did you not grasp that part, Ridley? Perhaps your advanced years are catching up with you."

Ridley colored, a bright pink stain swimming unflatteringly across his cheeks. "We were at Eton together, Mercer. I only have you by a year!"

Tristan propped his elbow on the table and dropped his chin to his fist. "Honestly, I don't recall."

"Ousted during your third term, weren't you? That *I* recall."

"Rusticated, not expelled. A six-month sojourn from classes." Tristan's smile was positively beatific. "I thought I had the composition for the perfect pyrotechnic, but magnesium is a fickle ingredient, I learned and quickly. Took me a year to pay off the damage to the laboratory. And my hair didn't grow back properly for *two.*" He dragged his hand through the luscious, overlong strands, dark and wild as the healthiest soil in England. "Burned it right off my head on one side and took part of an eyebrow with it."

Camille jammed her fist over her mouth a second too late. Her laugher, delighted and *real*, she recognized the difference, sweeping the room like a summer breeze as the tight knot her belly had been twisted in since she accepted Ridley's proposal unfurled. After a quick instant, Tristan laughed, too, deep and wonderfully, his gaze dusting her before his smile slipped, and he glanced into his lap for no reason she could fathom.

Disconcerted, she looked to the man she'd pledged to marry and away from the one who'd always made her blood kick a touch harder than required. No more dreams squandered on the Duke of Mercer. Eight years his junior, too young to be bothered with until it was too late. Now, he presented a complicated mix of pensiveness, ferocity, and defensive humor, the intensity he tried to hide bubbling just beneath the surface.

The duke needed someone patient enough to figure him out. Someone who hadn't given up on loving him long ago.

While her intended, the man she'd *chosen*, would take her as she was, an amateur botanist who uncouthly made money doing it, or not take her at all.

~

*H*e'd laughed.

For the first time in years.

Out loud, surrounded by a roomful of people. And not one of those fake chuckles he could conjure up like a mystic a vision, but a genuine release of amusement and...*pleasure*.

Tristan Tierney, Duke of Mercer, Viscount Wimble, Baron Easley, took a thoughtful drag on his cheroot and blew smoke into the frigid Yorkshire night. Longleat Manor's terrace was deserted except for the occasional jangle of Lady Fontaine's off-tune pianoforte and the whistle of the wind through the trees. The men had retreated to the billiard room for port and ribald conversation while the ladies had absconded to the drawing room for more decorous entertainment.

While he, the evening's guest of honor, had slipped away like a thief.

His hiding place? The side garden, resting against a low brick wall missing quite a few bricks, in a shadowy corner where no one would find him unless they were really looking. He'd decided to sneak away when the conversation turned to the rumor that the Prince Regent was going to bestow a medal of valor upon him. Better to face the cold than the war, which is what Lady Fontaine's entire gathering, for their *leisure*, wanted him to do. The mere notion of telling anyone about those days made him queasy.

At this moment, he wished only to be the Duke of Mercer, number five.

Simple that, in comparison.

Tristan tilted his head to gaze at the heavens. A crystal-clear night, an endless expanse of black velvet pinholed with a thousand stars. He'd lain beneath such a sky while surrounded by men he'd lead into battle the next day, many of whom would not return. When he'd fled Yorkshire with the desire to become a man under his own direction, he'd had no idea what death looked like, what fear that gripped you from the bone *felt* like.

How fragile life truly was.

However, he wasn't going to think about the damned war right now. Enveloped by a frosty twilight and the wine he'd pilfered from the kitchens, he was going to allow alcohol to quietly cloud his mind while he fantasized about his best friend's sister.

While he'd been away, Camille Bellington had become a woman.

A gorgeous, intelligent, defiant woman.

With a husky voice hinting at raging hearthfires and eyes an unusual blue-green, like a stormy sea one couldn't help but dive into. Her slender body wrapped in a shimmering confection of ivory silk, a fillet of pearls slinking through her russet strands, he'd been tempted to remove her gown—and those pearls—with his teeth.

He released a tense breath and took a slug straight from the bottle. He needed a woman, *any* woman but the one who'd sparked his interest this eve, and if he weren't afraid of falling asleep after the act and waking in the middle of a blinding nightmare, he would've already found one.

As it was, he'd been alone for what seemed like forever.

"A botanist," he whispered into the night. With a grin he guessed was getting wobbly at the edges, he chuckled against the bottle's neck. How extraordinarily dreadful in the most charming way. No wonder she'd been left behind when less worthy women had been snapped up. Beautiful and spirited and housing actual *intellect* behind a shy smile, she must have tossed the men of the *ton* on their arses the instant they asked a question and she provided a clever answer.

He'd not known this about her, the love of plants and such. Though he did recall finding pressed flowers hidden between the pages of his schoolbooks. He'd pop one open in the middle of a lecture, and a squashed daisy or crumpled rose would tumble out. Pushing the heel of his hand into his eye, he tried to recall. She'd been precocious. Annoying, like a burr under his skin. Talkative, too curious, a pest. He'd brushed her off—and away—a thousand times. She had to be eight, nine, ten years his junior, for God's sake. A pretty child, an attractive girl.

And now…

His cock did a disturbing dance beneath his trouser close.

Oh, no, Tris. No.

Then the terrace door clicked, and there she was, the precocious, delectable Lady Bellington, standing in a spill of moonlight that dripped off the pearls in her hair and did a delicious slide down her body.

She was tall. Tall enough for him to do glorious things to her while standing up. In fact, the wall he rested alongside was a magical height for certain activities.

"Christ," he whispered and knocked his head against brick.

She stepped to the edge of the terrace. "Who's there?" Four marble steps and fifteen-odd feet, and she'd stumbled right across him.

He chuckled—another surprise when he'd believed amusement long dead—and spoke before he could stop himself. "I'm sorry about the swan story, Princess. It was a diversion from the things they wanted." Grinning, he gestured with the bottle. "It's just, I've never seen someone totally covered in mud, head to toe, and battling a violently angry swan. I smile every time I think about it. Which I'm sure says something base about my character."

She frowned; he saw this clearly when a stray moonbeam struck her face. Then she shook her head, blew out a half-breath, and smiled right back at him. To say his response to that show of wit was like a jarring blow to the solar plexus would have been an understatement.

Proving her mettle, and lack of discretion, she pranced down the steps and to his concealed spot as if being alone with a man of his reputation was a fine idea. "You sound foxed, Your Grace."

Tristan brought the bottle to his lips and watched her through olive green glass as he drank. Either this or give in to the insane urge to kiss her. "Not quite there, but I'm trying."

"Why?"

He halted, staring up at her, incredulous she'd ask. If she was going to *'your grace'* him, did she really want to know? "Because they want a piece I'm not willing to share," he finally said through clenched teeth, a statement he was astounded he uttered.

She tilted her head, chewed on what looked to be a plump lower lip, held out her hand. "Your greatcoat, if you don't mind."

He sat up, stunned but accommodating, and wrestled his sleeves off his arms. Giving it to her, he shrugged as if to say, *now what?* She had on a voluminous cloak herself, her body swaddled in woolen folds.

With a playful smile, Camille spread his coat out like a blanket, and in a relaxed move, settled next to him without flashing so much as a hint of ankle. "I didn't prepare for a picnic, and this color of silk is unforgiving," she said and gestured to her gown. Grabbing the bottle from his hand, she took a dainty sip. Ran her tongue along her teeth, then took another, deeper this one.

He studied her profile, moonlight turning the ends of her eyelashes gold, and a haunting tightness deep inside him released, like a lock being sprung. "I'm not going to talk about it."

She wagged the bottle in his direction. "No need."

He inhaled to clear his mind, bringing in the scent of peony and a dash of orange blossom. The air surrounding her was suggestive of English summers, and for some bloody reason, freedom. "I visited a rifleman's family yesterday on my way here, a man under my leadership. He lived in Stamford, a staging point for the London to York coaches, so a convenient stop for my carriage and crew. I told this young man's mother how he'd fought and bravely perished on a field in the Netherlands during Wellington's war. La Haye Sainte was where we staged that final battle. Sounds regal, doesn't it, when it was just a farm. And Daniel Larson, just a boy."

She turned and stared until he was forced to face her. An owl called out, and the wind whispered between them. His heart ached, and he had no idea how to ease the pain. He reached for the bottle, but she shoved it behind her back. "Pretend I'm Edward or someone in your regiment you'd confide in. Say what you feel you can't but must." She brought her knees up and propped her cheek atop them, gazing out across the distance, letting his heart settle without her direct regard. "Sometimes, when I'm rooting a new species of plant, I talk, and the words reveal the answer, the how and why. The sound of my voice relieves the pressure and the mystery. Maybe you could try it. We were family friends of a sort once."

So he did. Talked until his fingers were numb from the cold, until he imagined his nose was as red as the holly berries Camille had sprinkled across her aunt's dining table. Talked until, like the girl who'd fought a swan in the Serpentine said he might, he felt the slightest release of the bands strapped around his chest.

The sound of footsteps on the terrace had them both glancing toward the house.

Tristan grabbed her arm before she rose, her pulse skipping where his gloved thumb covered her wrist. The fast tick belied the serene expression on her face. On a spurt of panic at their diminishing time, he said, "This hobby, your plants. I'm staying the night at your aunt's invitation. Tomorrow, after breakfast, you could show me."

"It's a business," she corrected and wiggled her arm from his grip.

"Despite what Ridley thinks."

She snorted inelegantly while rising elegantly to her feet.

Handed him his bottle and his coat. "*Despite* what the viscount thinks. He'll have to get used to it."

The idea of Ridley getting used to anything Camille Bellington dished out caused a twinge he'd best ignore to swim through Tristan's belly. "Your grandfather's conservatory? Is that where you conduct your business? I can meet you there. I remember where it is."

She started toward the house, mumbling something that sounded like *'not chasing a duke'* beneath her breath before glancing back over her shoulder. "Why, Your Grace, would you be interested in botany?"

I'm not. I'm only interested in you. Instead, he said, "My father's garden is in terrible distress. Consider it an interview. More business for Bellington Botany at the ducal estate down the way. Imagine how old Ridley will turn eleven shades of crimson when he hears about it."

Her smile was amazing to observe, unfolding like one of her blasted flowers. "I shouldn't like that so much, but I do."

Tristan rose to his feet, his head still light from the wine. "Tomorrow morning, then?"

"I'm not sure it's a good idea."

He blinked, utterly unused to being denied. "Why not?"

"All you used the conservatory for was kissing back in the day. It's a respectable place of business now. What would the flowers think?"

"*What?*"

Her laugh broke free, a sound as intoxicating as her balmy scent, in such contrast to the winter night. "Victoria Primrose. Remember?"

He muscled his hand through his hair, searching his memory. *Ah*, yes. "Blasted hell, I couldn't have been more than fifteen. A bet with Edward. It wasn't good, the kiss. I had no idea what I was doing. She certainly never asked me to repeat it." With a shiver, he worked his arms back into his coat. "You must have had your nose pressed to a dirty pane to see the sad performance."

"And you do now," Camille murmured around a smile. "Have an idea of what to do."

He tipped the bottle her way. "Care to find out, Princess?"

The split-second pause, barely perceptible if he weren't searching for it, made his heart, unbelievably, soar. "No," she whispered, "I wouldn't."

But as he watched her walk away, he could only cheerfully think, *by God, I don't believe you.*

CHAPTER 2

Where a kiss kills.

Camille startled with every sound, every creak, tick, or shift when the conservatory was her safe place. Her peaceful domicile. She frowned and brushed her hand across her cheek, glad, yes, *glad* she'd worn her oldest dress and smashed straw bonnet, misshapen after her maid, Annabelle, sat on it last week. She didn't want Tristan Tierney of all people to think anything about this meeting, even if they'd flirted, *mildly* flirted, the evening before. He'd been foxed, and she bored, or rather, frustrated. With Ridley.

Which was becoming a common occurrence.

Morning, the duke had said. *I'll meet you in the morning.* When morning meant anything from eight o'clock to two in the afternoon. Camille enjoyed rising early, unlike most of society. She couldn't imagine Tristan waking before noon.

She was not getting involved with him beyond this conference, she pledged right there with her hand buried in fresh, flaky peat. Even if he'd told her shockingly private things in her aunt's enchanting garden the evening prior, brought images from his mind of loneliness and death and destruction—and placed them firmly in hers.

Even *if*.

She exhaled and wedged her hip against the wooden bench housing her pots and jars and vases. Tools, sacks of seed. Warped shelves lined with plants and cuttings. A sunlit shimmer danced through the greenhouse wall to dust her face. She closed her eyes and drew a loamy breath into her lungs, the smell of moss and freshly-turned earth settling her as it always did.

The Duke of Mercer, more than any man alive, was her weakness. It didn't matter why or how, but she'd been utterly, irretrievably in love with him since, well, she couldn't remember when she *hadn't* been in love with him.

So, it had been forever.

Forever, when he'd treated her like a child. Because she'd *been* a child. The mere mention of his name enough to send a dizzyingly twist through her belly when she'd never been a foolish female. Unless he was involved.

When she experienced nothing like that with Ridley. Pleasant, accommodating Ridley, whom she *liked* but didn't love.

Which she was as pleased about as she was her choice of bland gardening attire.

Her matrimonial selection had been made in opposition to her fascination with a beguiling man far from reach. Simpler to say, she wanted to be the one who loved *less*. The control in that decision felt marvelous. She would be a very proper, most agreeable wife, aside from her botany fixation.

Which was acceptable, as she suspected Ridley didn't love her, either.

But her fiancé's gaze warmed when he looked at her, a

hunger she could appease. A reliable business arrangement, his funds for her ability to provide a family to continue his line. It happened every day in society. Why she felt hesitation about the union was nothing short of ridiculous. She'd known she would someday commit to someone, and the bill collectors had decided it must be soon.

Another minute passed, maybe two, when a demanding footfall sounded on the gravel path leading to the conservatory. Camille smoothed her dress, tugged the flattened bonnet from her head, then, with a sigh, tossed it aside and made herself focus on pruning her potted plumeria.

But she couldn't keep herself from tilting her head and watching the Duke of Mercer saunter into her space as if he owned it. Casually dressed this morning in a cambric shirt, cravat loose, shirt open at the neck, he looked approachable, relaxed. Buckskin breeches clinging with each flex of his muscular thighs. And tall. Had he always been so tall he had to duck when he entered rooms?

Vexed, she squeezed the pruning shears in her fist. Oh, devil take it! Why fight what *was*? He was gorgeous. And witty. Intelligent and occasionally vulgar. Vulnerable, as he'd been the night before. Arrogant. Impatient.

Good and bad.

The hopelessness was, she loved the entire package.

Tristan glanced around as he traveled the row leading to her, a curious gaze, an interested one. Pausing by a tree, he circled his broad palm around a plum and plucked it free. Tossing her a jaunty look, he dusted the pink-red fruit on the sleeve of his shirt and noisily bit into it, a masculine show of bravado that made her toes curl inside her scuffed boots. "Damn," he whispered, raising it to his mouth for a second bite, "what is this?"

His tongue slid out to catch a drop of nectar, and she knew she was in dire trouble. She shouldn't want to close the short distance between them and kiss the juice off his lips, not when her experience equaled exactly two forgettable tryouts with her fiancé. She shouldn't know what she was missing, but somehow, she did. "A plum. This particular variety was discovered in a Sussex garden last year and is just entering the nursery trade. Not even officially named yet. By spring, it will be so laden with fruit, I'll have to prop up the branches."

He hummed softly beneath his breath, moving in until he stood close enough for her to see a stubbled spot on his jaw his valet had missed. Close enough to catch the scent of sandalwood and soap clinging to his skin. Chewing thoughtfully, he circled a sketch on the bench into his view. "Am I to receive the grand tour, then?"

She released the shears and stepped back, giving herself breathing room to assess his mood. Playful, the dark slashes beneath his eyes lighter than they'd been the night before; he'd gotten decent sleep for the first time in days, it seemed. "If you want one."

His gaze settled on her, this morning a mottled mix of light and dark green. He swallowed and took a deep bite of the plum. "I want one."

So she waded in deeper and shared her lone passion with a duke. A walking tour of her grandfather's conservatory. Her books, drawings, soil, fertilizer, tools. Potted experiments in cross-pollination. Efforts to grow species unaccustomed to Yorkshire. She shared as she would with another botanist as they walked the rows, from one long end of the musty building to the other. She shared in a way Ridley had never asked her to. In a way no one had asked her. It was quite something to open your heart and allow the private pieces to tumble out for casual viewing.

Ignoring the frisson of delight in her belly, she focused instead on the frisson of delight in her *mind*.

When she finished, they stood by the side door, where she kept the shrubs ready for delivery to Longleat's garden. Dusting her hands together, she focused on looking anywhere but at Tristan, unsure what to say to get him trotting back to the house and away from her.

"You're too good for Ridley. Too intelligent, too accomplished, too *everything*. You must know this."

Her head snapped up. The blasted man was fiddling with an azalea she'd had to nurse back to health without a hint of remorse for making such a bold statement. "How dare you say such a thing!"

"Why shouldn't I dare? Someone has to. Your aunt seems mute on the subject. And Edward doesn't appear to be involved. Did he agree to this?"

"My brother is in London, newly married himself, managing his affairs. Money is, unfortunately, scarce for him as well. I'm not letting Longleat leave this family when I can step in and save it. I wasn't forced into this arrangement. I made my own choice. Ridley was *my* choice."

"Somehow, Princess, that makes it worse."

"Stop calling me that." Camille strode past him, heading for the plumeria she needed to get back to pruning. "Hypocrite. As if you'd recognize a suitable duchess if you were hit atop the head with her. I can't wait to see who you select for the magnanimous position, Your Grace. Let me row my boat, will you?"

After a prolonged silence, Camille looked back to find him frowning as he knocked his boot against a wooden cart currently housing straw to be spread about the estate. "Don't tell me you've never considered it, Tris. You must deliver an heir someday. You're thirty now or thereabouts. It's time."

He paused, and she realized she'd uttered a nickname only her brother had used. It brought them closer than they'd ever been—with both of them finally of an age to do something about it.

"Thirty-one, June first." He took the last bite of plum with little enthusiasm. "And…I've thought about it. Running for my life through muddy fields in Belgium, I thought about a lot of things."

"Well, there. That's good. You're ready," she said and snipped the end of a plumeria branch off with more force than required, hating every suitable woman in England. "Excellent."

Tristan glanced from her hands to her face with an assessing look that sent a quiver of trepidation through her. His smile started small but grew as the seconds slipped between them, the sigh of the wind against greenhouse glass the only sound besides their hushed breaths.

"Oh, no." She shook her shears at him, a stabbing get-back motion. "I don't care who you pick. It's none of my affair. Nothing, nothing at all, to do with me. I'm taken, my decision made. Remember us rowing our own boats."

With a flick of his wrist, he tossed the plum pit into the rubbish bin in the corner and advanced on her. "You know, once upon a time, Edward believed you rather fancied me." He scrubbed his wrist across his lips, his grin disappearing behind his starched sleeve. "Of course, I was too old for you, already away at Cambridge. What is it between us? Nine years?"

Camille bumped back into the bench, rocking it into the wall. "Eight."

He danced his fingers over a gerbera leaf, a tea rose's stem. "Even better."

"There is no better," she rushed out as he closed in on her. "There's nothing."

He halted before her, trying mightily to contain his amusement, but his mouth kept turning up. She ground her teeth and dug her bootheel into the stone floor. What amused him, she'd love to know.

"How did you test old Ridley anyway?"

"Test? What test?"

Gingerly removing the shears from her hand, Tristan laid them aside and pressed his lips together, cutting hideously appealing groves beneath his cheeks. *Who should have a face such as this and it not be carved in marble*, she wondered furiously? "A kiss. Was that it? To decide if Ridley was the man for you. It must have been a good one. Surprising, because he doesn't seem the persuasive type." He trailed his index finger along her cheek and into her hair. "A spiderweb." With a light tug, he pulled the silken thread out and flicked it loose—and her knees went weak with yearning.

She watched it flutter to the ground with an escalating sense of dread.

"There was no kiss," she whispered, her voice frayed with a needful edge he was not likely to miss. She exhaled softly, defeated. "No good kiss." Rather, there'd only been a mediocre one. No, two. A mediocre *two*. But admitting this was like throwing a gauntlet of some sort at Tristan's feet when he already had the cunning look of a man trying to solve a puzzle.

He tipped her chin high with a laugh that sent a plum-scented puff sliding across her cheek. "I notice you didn't deny the fancying me rumor, Princess."

She swayed, placing her hand on his chest to steady herself. His placid expression disguised his violent heartbeat.

The theory ripped through her like a harrowing winter gust. *He's affected by me, too.*

Finally.

"What's that look?" He moved to frame the nape of her neck, stepped in, knee bumping hers, his other hand going to her waist, gently pulling her in without a hint of ownership.

Loss of control she'd have fought. His pupils flared, flooding his eyes black. "It almost looks like triumph." He leaned in as his lids fluttered. "Now, why is that?"

Camille realized lifting on her toes to reach him, the one man in the world who could break her into a thousand pieces, was a mistake. Realized skidding her hand over his broad shoulder, into his tousled strands, and drawing his lips to hers was another one.

She wasn't even sure who kissed whom first.

She wasn't sure what to *do*.

But he knew. And she followed.

Cradling her jaw, he tilted her head, arranging, like he'd done it a thousand times before, walking her back into the bench with a swift step. His ragged sigh, needful and anguished, dispelled her uncertainty like dew in harsh sunlight. Deliberately, gently, his mouth molded to hers, coaxing, pleading without words, a query not a demand, his tongue sweeping inside when she parted her lips on a low, surrendering gasp.

It was a tender kiss, a slow burn. And when it started to move faster, his arm circled her waist, and he swept her against his long, hard body.

Swept her into a miraculous world she'd dreamt about but never experienced.

His scent surrounded her as his taste became hers. The smell of frost and plums, cinnamon and tea, the flavor of passion, promise, *yearning*. She tangled her hand in his hair and arched into him, seeking more. *More*. She even whispered it, a breathy pant into his mouth that seemed to make him crazy, make him clutch her, hard, devouring her like he was parched and she cool, sparkling water. Sparks danced behind her eyelids, as bright as the pop of magnesium. From shoulder to hip, they were one. His pulse dancing beneath her questing fingers, the rock of his hips, a pleasure punch generating a forbidden, heavy pressure between her thighs.

She'd never imagined anything like this.

But she'd been right about her attraction even if her craving had begun long before she could satisfy it.

His hand trailed from her waist, and she purred when he reached her ribcage, her nipple pebbling in anticipation of its first caress. *Yes, there.* Maybe she even whispered that, too.

Tristan pulled back just enough to gaze at her, his breath ripping from his lungs to bat her cheek. Her fingers were twisted in his hair; her other hand clenched around the cambric covering his shoulder. He looked wild, his eyes glowing the deepest green she'd ever seen them, his skin flushed, his lips rosy-red and abused.

Power of a variety unknown to her until that moment streaked through her.

"Don't," she whispered when he pulled away. *Not yet. Don't let this end yet.* She pressed her lips to his jaw and nibbled, softly, without reason, only knowing she wanted him, wanted this.

"I can't think," he rasped and took her by the shoulders, forcing her back in a startling move unlike his usual grace. For five hushed breaths, they stared, collecting reasons for staying, for going.

For breaking promises or making them.

Suddenly, like the shocking jab of a needle, she grasped what she was doing.

She was chasing the duke.

And thanks to her brother, the duke in question had always *known* she was chasing him.

She turned in a fury, presenting her back, considered sweeping the row of ceramic pots on the bench to the ground. "Go, Mercer. Leave, *now*." She pushed the heel of her hand against the thumping pulse at her neck. She'd never been so provoked in her life, never imagined the like. Her body aflame, vibrating with each beat of her heart. Her knees threatening to betray her.

And Ridley, dear heaven, what to do about Ridley?

Tristan sighed and stepped back. His footfall cracked the straw scattered over the stone floor. "May I have a moment to catch up without you getting angry? The kiss...I didn't know...I didn't expect..."

"Oh, bother, *please*. Considering your reputation, I assumed you'd be better at the après portion of this."

He sighed again, this sound less forgiving, for which of them, she'd no clue. "Is it true, what Edward said? About you fancying me? That's all I'm asking. I'm trying to put the pieces in place with, admittedly, half a mind at present."

Glancing over her shoulder, she schooled her features into what she hoped was a bland expression while blood sprinted violently through her veins. "It was. Does that make you happy? And why, pray tell, at this late stage of the game, should it matter? You were my childhood fantasy of the perfect man. My heart galloped when you were in the same room. I staged a thousand silly plays with you as the hero." She smiled, and she had no mirror, but it felt bitter. "But it was long ago, Your Grace. I grew up. And you left."

His eyes flashed, his hands going into fists at his side. "I had to leave. And I'm no one's hero."

She lifted her head to stare out the streaked, stained greenhouse glass. "I suppose you're right. Or we're both wrong, take your pick."

"Somehow, I've gone from wanting to tear your clothes off to wanting to spank you." He laughed harshly and banged his boot against the bench. "Which can be done in the same session actually."

"That's revolting." Wasn't it?

"Princess, don't judge until you've tried it."

Goosebumps danced along her skin at his velvet tone and the lurid images flooding her mind. She dropped her head to her hand. "Go away, Tristan, go away and leave me in peace."

"I can't believe I'm going to say this, I can't believe I feel it..." He blew a breath between his teeth. "But I don't want to. I think I want to talk. About, well, *us*."

"There is no us. I'm marrying Ridley, or have you forgotten? The creditors have left me no choice, or virtually none, regarding the timing."

He twisted a barberry leaf from the bush at his side and traced his finger along the vein. "I have another question. Just one, and I'll leave you to your plants. Was his kiss *anything* like mine?"

She curled her arm around her belly and leaned into her amusement. "You must be joking. That's not a fair assessment. The man has kissed one woman to your one hundred! An amateur compared to a master."

"You're exaggerating the state of affairs. And you don't need to make excuses for him. Or me. Although in a roundabout way, I suppose your response answers my question."

Turning to face him, she dropped to rest her bottom on the wide window ledge. The glass was warm from the sun when she leaned against it. A golden ray pocketed the opportunity to trip across Tristan, turning the tips of his hair amber, shooting unneeded brilliance into his startling emerald eyes. It was a crime to be so handsome, it honestly was. "I don't need kisses that kill, Your Grace. In fact..." She picked at her gown's ratty hem and shrugged. "I don't even want them."

He glanced away, chewing on the inside of his cheek, his jaw ticking in anger. "Is this punishment because I didn't know about your infatuation? You were too young. I'm glad I didn't heed Edward's chatter. God knows what I might have done the first time I got a true look at the grown-up you."

"I made a promise when you left that I wasn't going to chase you anymore. In my mind, in my heart. I'm sorry you're only now finding out about it. Perhaps the timing is inconvenient."

His gaze came back to hers, the leaf dropping from his hand. "So you'll marry Ridley with this between us? Without even questioning what nearly happened here? I can't explain it, either, but I think it might *mean* something. Maybe we take a step back to reflect?"

She tilted her head in question, truly curious. "Are you offering another option?"

Yanking his fingers through his hair and leaving it in charming spikes, he snapped, "I don't know what the bloody hell I'm offering. When you so neatly bit my jaw with your lovely little teeth, thought raced from my mind like a runaway stallion. I'm stunned, dumbfounded, *brainless*, Lady Bellington, because this was supposed to be a tranquil Yorkshire Christmas!"

The sound of a hinge squealing had Tristan taking a fast step back with a muttered *'brilliant'* sliding in beneath his breaths. Countess Milburn and Viscount Ridley stood in the conservatory's entrance, similar banal expressions on their faces.

Camille retrieved her shears and snipped a length of plumeria. "Certainly, Your Grace. After the holiday, I'll schedule a consultation to look at Tierney Hall's gardens. I'm sure, even if it's only providing replacement shrubs and trees, I can work with your gardener to get the estate in better shape." She flicked her fingers at him as she would an errand boy as his fist clenched at his side. "Thank you for considering me. You're right, I do good work."

"*Very* good," he whispered, gave her a tight bow that said, *this isn't over*, and strode through the greenhouse's back door without speaking to her intended or the countess.

"Uncivilized beast, isn't he?" Ridley strolled down center aisle. He didn't stop to look at anything, passing the plum tree Tristan had taken such delight in without a glance. Camille understood there was meaning in this comparison, but her heart wasn't up to the tally. "War ruined him, ruined them all. Not fit for society. It's better if he inhabits his crumbling ducal estate in the next village and never leaves. Plenty of work for two lifetimes getting that place in shape from what I've heard, although he has the blunt, lucky man. Town certainly doesn't need such boorish behavior. We have too much as it is." He grasped Camille's hand when he reached her, a proprietary touch bringing none of the fever Tristan's had. "Darling, we need to talk about this botany business."

Camille looked him in the eye, refusing to cower. Although her family needed funds, she would provide an heir, so they were negotiating critical elements on both sides. "I'm happy you finally agree it's a business."

"What's this about Mercer hiding out for the rest of his life in the country?" Countess Milburn saddled up next to Ridley with a knowing simper. "Stunning, wealthy dukes are welcome anywhere and everywhere, Ridley dear, and they always will be." She winked and laid her finger atop the bow of her lip. "Isn't that right, Lady Camille?"

Camille looked into eyes the exact color of an English oak's bark and wondered what the countess had seen on her face as the Duke of Mercer stalked from her conservatory?

Heartache? Regret?

Because she'd wanted nothing more than to beg him to stay.

CHAPTER 3

Where a tree is slain and an attraction suppressed.

Camille didn't want a kiss that killed.

Tristan tugged his gloves on and flexed his fingers inside the supple, black kidskin. Well, *he* did. And as of this morning, ten minutes after rising and guzzling his first cup of tea, he'd decided he wasn't leaving Yorkshire as soon as he'd planned after receiving one.

Not with that honest, raw, beautiful moment they'd shared jabbing him in the gut and shouting, *good God, man, go get her.*

He'd never been more shocked by his reaction or a woman's response. A most delicious and unexpected surprise. The two of them, he and Camille, why, they'd been like that preposterous chemistry experiment that had blown up in his face at Eton. Except this had been a successful endeavor, an explosion of the best kind. A sizzle beneath his skin and in his blood he'd been unable to tamp down. The compulsion to *touch*, without plan, without purpose, had been overwhelming and instantaneous. One moment, he'd been diving into eyes the color of the North Sea, the next, he'd found himself with an armful of delectable, orange-blossom-scented woman.

His dreams the previous night had demonstrated he was on the right track with this kissing business. They'd featured Camille and Camille only, alabaster skin flushed, head thrown back as she cried out his name, legs, long ones he'd noticed while sucking on a plum in her conservatory, wrapped firmly about his waist. *Tris*, she'd called out. A name a lover had never spoken. He wouldn't have allowed it.

For the first time in months, dreams of war hadn't been part of his slumber.

Consequently, here he was, standing in the foyer of Lady Fontaine's country manor, waiting on a group of people to go on a hunt for a Christmas tree, whatever *that* was, his mind full of a kiss and those dreams—his cock hard as stone beneath buckskin, a circumstance, if it did not soon diminish, he'd be forced to hide.

All because of a woman he'd not known he needed.

A woman who'd wanted him once, when he hadn't known to want her back.

An intelligent, beautiful, spirited woman recently engaged to a bloke Tristan felt sure he didn't like.

Tristan had no idea what to do about that. About any of it. But he wasn't leaving Isabel Fontaine's home until he figured it out.

"Still here, Mercer? No one to debauch in London?"

He turned to find Viscount Ridley tottering down the grand staircase, a bulging portmanteau clutched in his fist. Tristan grinned. This day was getting better and better. "No, I've determined a longer visit at Longleat Manor is in order. Family friends and all. You know, I spent many a day here with Lady Camille's brother, Edward." He yawned, then nodded to Ridley's luggage. "Looks like you're haring back to Town, however."

Ridley halted alongside Tristan, dropped his bag to the faded Aubusson, and snaked his gloves from his pocket. "My mother," he said and jerked them on with a grunt. "I have to get back to her before Christmas, you know."

"And leave your intended?"

Ridley paused, his smile dimming. "Well, Lady Camille's with family. And she has her plants," he muttered the complaint with less volume. "Plenty to keep her occupied. Countess Milburn's ball, festivities in the village, and so on. I'll see her soon. We've got to make plans, you see. Have the banns read. Plan the parties."

"She has me to entertain, or be entertained by, you could also say." A smidgen like stepping into a ring, this admission, a ring Tristan wasn't sure he wanted to step into. In all honesty, he didn't know what this meant for him, Camille, or Ridley, his deciding to stay for the holiday. Still, he wanted the man to acknowledge he was leaving his betrothed with a family friend, sure, but not a brother.

A family friend who'd found he carried an undeniable attraction for the betrothed in question. A family friend who, at times, had been correctly labeled a bounder.

Ridley looked up into Tristan's face, searching. At times like these, Tristan was glad for his height. "Ah, hmm, I think I'll stay for the tree cutting at least. A new tradition started in Germany, the countess told me, even though I think it's dangerous. Fire hazard and all. Don't need to rush back to London just yet. Mother will understand a slight delay."

"Your mother likes Lady Camille I assume? Excited about the marriage?"

Ridley's cheeks paled. "She'll be thrilled. Absolutely." He coughed into his cupped fist and did a nervous sidestep that said he wasn't as sure as he sounded. "When I tell her. Which I will. By January first, no later. Thrilling news for a new year. I'm her only son, you know. One must wade into these topics gently."

Tristan tilted his head as steps sounded on the floor above, signaling the rest of the group was marching downstairs. "For you, I hope so."

Ridley raised a brow. "Why wouldn't Mother be excited?"

Tristan snatched his greatcoat from the hall stand and shrugged into it. "Oh, no reason." Working bottom to top, he buttoned while hiding his mirth behind a look of concern. "Lady Camille's a bit of a hoyden. Independent. A handful, if you must know. Always has been. Didn't you listen to the swan story? And her talk about botany? A fierce intellect housed inside a comely package. A sharp blade wrapped in rose petals, as it were." Smoothing his lapels, he rolled his shoulders into the coat's excellent fit. "I hope you're prepared to manage her *and* your mother as men must when they marry. You've stepped high, my man, with your selection."

Ridley snorted and reached for his own coat. "Mistresses more your passion, aren't they, Mercer? Talk about low stepping. What was the last one, an actress?"

Tristan frowned and gave Ridley credit for getting in a verbal nick. Then he turned at the sound of laughter and grasped he should have been worrying about his festering attraction to Camille, not trading barbs with her idiot husband-to-be.

Because she was exquisite. And he was in trouble.

Seemingly lost in thought, Camille trailed behind her aunt and Countess Milburn as they descended the circular staircase, her fingers stroking the banister as she floated along.

She wore another patched gown that looked like it should be given to the rag-and-bone man when he came to collect clothing, but the faded muslin, once canary yellow, he guessed and now somewhere closer to the color of wheat, molded to her delicate curves. As his hands had been starting to in her stale conservatory the morning prior. Her hair was collected in a loose chignon, wisps escaping to dust her cheek and temple. It looked like a hairstyle she'd adopted after crawling from bed, a consideration which didn't help his state of arousal. At all.

He couldn't keep his gaze from dropping to the curve of her breast, slight but utterly adequate, jiggling with each step she took. Yesterday, he had stopped himself before he set his broad palm there, over the delectable nipple stabbing through her bodice.

He'd stopped himself because that was going too far with a naïve, young woman. When he'd wanted to roll the hard nub beneath his thumb more than he'd wanted his next breath. In the dream still haunting him, he'd taken it between his teeth and made her cry out until she was breathless, taken a handful of her thick, golden-brown hair and gathered it in his fist as he slid into her welcoming body.

With an oath, Tristan snatched his beaver hat from the hall stand and placed it over his erection before anyone, *God, please, not Ridley*, noticed his dilemma.

Camille ignored him on her journey across the foyer when he knew she knew he was there. She graced Ridley with a smile as he assisted with her fur-lined pelisse, and he returned it with a genuineness that gave Tristan's gut a firm twist. He sighed and tapped the hat against his thigh. The viscount, dullard that he was, was besotted. Who could blame him? Wearing a years-old frock, her hair a fright, her smile on this side of devious, she was lovely. And interesting. Clever. Tristan had never been involved with a clever woman. Shrewd ones. Beautiful ones. One here and there rather vile.

But not clever.

With a wicked gleam in her eye that said she was as unpredictable as he was. As sure of herself. As certain of who she *was*.

He'd never encountered such a woman.

"There are two types, old chap," Ridley whispered as if he'd read Tristan's mind. "Those you shag and those you read headlines from the *Times* to over tea and crumpets. Didn't think it was possible to want both with the same woman."

The wonder in Ridley's voice had Tristan furiously shoving his hat on his head, opening the front door, and stalking through it. The air was crisp when it hit his lungs, scented with woodsmoke and frost, the hills and dales of Yorkshire. It smelled like *home*. He gazed into the distance, over the fallow fields, guessing snow would be upon them by lunch. He loved winter, loved this section of England, wanted no part of London anymore. His estate, Tierney Hall, needed attention, care his father had not given it in years. Backbreaking work Tristan was looking forward to accomplishing. He should leave Longleat as planned, right this minute, before tromping through the forest with Camille for a tree to place *inside* the house, an outrageous tradition that had made its cozy way to England.

But instead he stood there on the veranda of Lady Fontaine's modest country manor, a home Camille was trading her future to save, while marveling that he, duke, soldier, rake, scoundrel, not in any particular order, was possibly, maybe, perhaps developing feelings for his best friend's little sister. Viscount Ridley's intended. *Yes, that one,* he thought and blew out an agitated breath.

Under normal circumstances, a duke beat a viscount any day of the week, but Camille was not—and this was part of his fasciation, he understood—a woman who took the sure bet.

What scared him the most?

The notion of leaving her in his bed and waiting for her to arrive at his breakfast table for tea, crumpets, and the *Times*.

It felt right, a circumstance he thought he'd rather enjoy.

Something, he could tell Ridley but wouldn't dare, he'd never desired with the same woman, either.

~

Tristan had misbuttoned his greatcoat. Near the top, leaving a bulge of wool she couldn't take her eyes off. Her fingertips tingled with the urge to repair.

So Camille did what she knew she shouldn't. Stopped the duke with a touch to his elbow as they entered the woodlands bordering Longleat Manor, letting the countess, her aunt, and Ridley move deeper into the pine thicket, her aunt giving her a playful wink that correctly assessed Camille's folly as she passed.

Tristan's cheeks, beneath the wide brim of his hat, were rosy, his breath fogging the air where it exited his lips. He carried the ax because they'd all quietly agreed he was highly capable, and he stood there gazing at her with a flat, undecipherable expression.

She gazed back, recording the changes. Faint lines streaking from his mouth, broader of face and body. A pale scar on his temple she assumed was from the war. Another beneath the line of his jaw. He shifted the ax from hand to hand, allowing the perusal, after a moment doing his own, his gaze scorching where it touched. Neck, waist, knees. A gradual slide to the tips of her boots, a gradual rise back. When his eyes returned to hers, the heat banked inside moss-green was marked.

"Are we going to stand here mentally stripping each other of clothing, or are you going to tell me what you want?"

She blinked, her stomach knotting as heat flooded her body. "I wasn't mentally stripping you of anything."

He dug the tip of the ax's blade into the moist earth. "Just me then. Apologies."

"Your coat," she said stupidly and gestured to the missed button.

He glanced down, a smile flexing the edges of his lips. "Ah," he said as if this wasn't a real reason. As if she'd done it to gain a private audience with him.

As if she'd done it so she could *touch* him.

"Never mind." She brushed past, the recognizable brand of embarrassment Tristan dished out as vexing as a hard pinch. "I simply wanted to correct a mistake, so you didn't look foolish in front of the others."

"My sartorial angel," he murmured and easily caught up to her. Taking her wrist in hand, insistent, he halted her step. "Come now, would you leave me thus, with my rig-out requiring emergency, in-field adjustment? I can't chop down some poor, helpless tree for your holiday pleasure with my buttons mismatched."

"Rascal," she whispered, but mirth undermined the word.

"Urchin," he returned with his own delight.

Oh, to hell with it she decided and put her hands on the Duke of Mercer.

As she'd been dying to all morning. All her *life*.

She didn't touch him any more than necessary, however, as she set about repairing the closure of his coat. Also, she kept her gaze focused on his chest while she worked and not a speck higher. Or lower. They didn't speak. She tried to ignore how his body had warmed the thick wool, and the way his minty breath brushed her temple in tepid bursts. Ignore how wonderful he smelled—of soap and nutmeg and oolong tea. Ignore the scrape of starched linen against his skin as he shifted to allow her better access.

But it was for naught. Awareness, hot and dazzling, traveled from her fingertips to her toes and back like it was on a track with no exit.

This was no kiss.

It was better. It was worse. It was maddening.

"Are you quite finished?" he asked in an uneven tone.

Her hands had fallen still, pressed into his woolen lapels. Snow was drifting in fat chunks around them. The air was thick, charged, molten. It felt like they were the only two people in the world. "Why did you decide to stay?" she asked and finally, *finally*, found the courage to look into his face, to note the thin black border circling his irises, specks of amber mixed in. His eyes were truly spectacular, and if he didn't have so many excellent features, she'd have said they were his best.

He swallowed hard and reached up to pull her hands down by her side though he didn't release her. "You may not know what we're doing, but I do. Where we're going with this." Glancing into the distance, he struggled to compose himself, then glanced back, his fierce gaze igniting a blaze in her belly. He tightened his hold, and his frantic pulse filtered into her consciousness. "Either I kiss you now like we both desperately want and you find it in yourself to tell Ridley something is happening between us, or we agree, right here in a snowy Yorkshire field, to take the safe bet and stop this. Back to being distant family friends, if we can, ending this before it gets away from us." He pulled her close, into his body, swore, laughed roughly, and released her. "Your confounded expression added to my confusion speaks volumes. And I know it's a surprise, trust me. I'm shocked, too, but it appears I'm not the cuckolding type. There's also my best friend to consider, a man I respect above all others, your protective older brother. While you…" He yanked his beaver hat from his head, threading his fingers through his dark strands in a show of pure frustration. "You're caught in a childish infatuation you don't know how to back out of. I'm not even sure your attraction is real. When mine is astonishingly genuine."

She opened her mouth to argue, then realized what she'd been about to say and stumbled back, out of his reach. "I have to save Longleat Manor, and my piddling botany efforts are no longer enough to do it. It's my home, my aunt's home, and she's too old to leave. I owe her, and she'd hate me saying it, for taking me in after my parent's carriage accident. I'm not fleeing to London to be a burden on Edward should that be your suggestion. In any case, I'd have nowhere in the city to house my plants, do my experiments. My notes, my books. Ridley will allow me to keep my work here, although I may have to insist he do so. You see, he's offering a solution to my problem, a solution a thousand women in the *ton* have taken before me, and I'm offering a solution to his."

"A loveless solution. On your side, at least. Why you're choosing him. He doesn't make you feel anything." He clicked his tongue against his teeth. "It's an admirable strategy. I'm not trying to suggest it isn't."

She laughed, shocked he would mention this. "What has love to do with marriage?"

Tristan bounced the ax on his boot, his face a study in bewilderment. "Nothing in my experience. My parents could barely stand to be on the same continent. And when they were, it was wretched. Why I was hiding out here so often if you must know."

Camille looked away before he witnessed sympathy crossing her face. He wouldn't welcome the emotion, and she didn't want to share it. Her heart was open like a tea rose in the spring, and she needed to distance herself until the petals closed.

Countess Milburn's laughter filtered by on a frigid gust, deciding for them.

Camille stepped around him and started across the field, sure, for some reason absolutely *sure*, the Duke of Mercer would follow.

~

"He left? Just up and left? Before dinner even?"

Camille made a note in her text on plant anatomy and lifted her gaze to her aunt, who stood in the doorway of Longleat's modest library with a scowl marring her patrician features. "Ridley had to get back to his mother, Aunt Bel. The dowager viscountess isn't comfortable being alone in the family townhome, although Grosvenor Square is the safest address in the city. And they employ a large staff as well. But who am I to judge? He *is* her only child."

"Men with too close a relationship to their mother are a disaster, love. The reason I turned down my fifth proposal. Lord Birley, I think it was. His mother was a fright. They slept in the same bed until he was twenty-one."

Camille laid her book and quill aside, realizing this conversation was going to occur, whether she wanted it to or not. Whether her aunt understood what she was talking about or not. Isabel Merchant, Lady Fontaine, daughter of a marquess and a steadfast bluestocking before they were titled as such, had never married, therefore had little practical experience with mother-in-laws.

Or rules.

Or impossibilities.

Strolling to the mahogany sideboard, Bel pulled the stopper off the brandy decanter, splashed a liberal amount in a tumbler, and took a brooding sip. "I'm not talking about Ridley, and you know it." Glancing over her shoulder, she gestured to her glass. "Would you like one?"

Camille nodded. She may as well get tipsy as the day had gone from bad to worse. Bad being trying to convince herself she didn't want to kiss Tristan again. Worse being watching him climb into his carriage and race into the night without a backward glance.

Typical of the way he handled conflict. *Run.*

Conversely, watching Ridley ride away had been painless.

Bel handed Camille a glass and took a precarious perch on the settee as if she expected to flutter off at any moment. The glow from the hearth rolled over her, an amber glimmer off her bone-gray chignon, her pewter eyes. "Did you see him handle that ax? The dainty English fur you selected for our holiday decor had no chance, two blows of the blade, and done. And he carried it back like it weighed nothing! Imagine a duke having such broad shoulders. Such muscles, no need for padding. His tailor must be impressed." She fanned her cheeks and blew out a honeyed breath. "My, did he grow up brilliantly. Celestial beauty. Simply celestial. While Ridley, poor devil, nearly chopped his toes off. Rather unfortunate, his masculine skills."

Camille slumped against the settee and rolled her head toward her aunt. "This is where this conversation is going? Talk of broad shoulders and the lack of muscle tone in my intended's arms?"

"So, you admit Mercer's attractive?" Bel laughed, a bawdy, booming laugh Camille associated with happiness and independence. Two things she was considering giving up. "What better topics than those, my darling botanist? Except for Ridley's lack of strength, that is. More interesting than"—she circled Camille's book into her line of sight, read the title, and visibility shuddered—"plant anatomy."

Camille traced her tongue over her teeth and took a healthy sip. "Of course, Mercer's attractive. I'm not blind."

"I wondered if you still thought so, because at one time you had your eye on him. Anytime he was in the same room, you were like a hawk over a mouse. It was quite captivating to watch."

"I was twelve years old, Bel. It was annoying."

Her aunt whistled through her teeth, releasing a refined, one-shouldered shrug. "Children are very wise, I've found. They see the truth when others can't. And a girl's infatuation compares not to a woman's. He may no longer be annoyed." She sipped and smiled, gazing about the room as if her next query wasn't a zinger. "While we're on this topic, might it have to do with you, his abrupt departure? The duke was extremely stoic during the tree-killing, those smiles he tosses out like tattered socks nowhere to be found. A foul mood, if I had my guess. He usually makes an effort to contain the darkness. And I used to know the boy well, quite well indeed."

Camille's mind, soothed by spirits, drifted. "I'm sure you did. He was here often when we were children."

Bel rotated the strand of pearls anxiously around her neck. They clinked softly, as only pearls can, gleaming in the candlelight. It was the last piece of jewelry left in the family; they'd sold the rest to keep the estate solvent. "Loneliest boy I've ever seen. His parents were unfit to *be* parents. A blessing they only had one child to ruin. Mercer's father was not a pleasant man. And his mother, ah, I wonder if it's unkind to say she was worse? Even without your parents, you had me. You had Edward. He had no one."

Camille glanced out the library window and watched snow stick to the glass pane. Tristan didn't have far to travel. Tierney Hall was less than five miles away. She hoped the roads were passable. Her parent's carriage had overturned no more than two miles from here on a snowy night twenty years ago. "His last mistress was the most famous actress in England," she murmured. "He's not lonely, Bel."

"You think lovers keep someone from being lonely?" Bel patted her hand and sighed as she dropped her head back to the settee. Her aunt's favored fragrance, jasmine with the lightest touch of lemon, drifted away from her with the movement. "How sweet, how naïve, when nothing is further from the truth. I should know. Lying next to someone you don't love can be a dreadfully forlorn experience. I'm trying to make you understand, in my delicate way, before it's too late."

Camille cringed and brought her arm over her face. She'd known her aunt had male friends years ago, but to discuss them was a different matter altogether. And thinking about Tristan in bed with another woman made her want to smash her tumbler against the wall. "I'm sure I don't want to hear this."

Bel turned to face her niece, grasped her hand, and held on tight. "I won't allow you to marry Ridley to save Longleat, Camille. Do you hear me? We can go to London. It might even be the best solution. You'll marry for love or not at all. I hoped if Mercer spent time with you, your infatuation would rise up and knock him in the head, now that you're old enough to act on it. You've both turned out so well, so pleasingly pretty, and he a hero, a difficult but good man. I will say, he couldn't remove his gaze from you today, though he tried mightily to. I'm surprised Ridley didn't challenge him, but he knows better. Mercer would thrash him, the pup."

"Maybe I love Ridley," Camille muttered after finishing the last of her brandy. Her head and belly were as warm as a lit ember, and she suddenly felt quite talkative. And sleepy.

Bel's gasp didn't disappear behind the hand she threw to her lips. "*Do you?*"

"I'm not chasing a duke. Never, ever, *ever* again."

Her aunt groaned and dropped her head. "I know he brought up the swan story, a bit cheeky, the naughty boy, but it's a fond remembrance among family."

Camille snorted, switched glasses with Bel and emptied it.

"Oh, darling"—she wrestled the crystal away from Camille—"you're going to be foxed."

Camille leaned back, closed her eyes, and imagined what it would be like to do more than kiss a man—when the kisses themselves were so, *so* good. Her mind swam with suggestive images that sent hot streaks along her skin. "He kisses like a demon. Horribly addictive, I imagine. Like opium. Absinthe even."

Bel sputtered a laugh. "Oh, dear, me, you *are* half-sprung. This is the greatest conversation of my life. Do go on."

"He has an enviable bottom lip I shall cling to next time. I think he'd like that. He didn't rush it, didn't force me. It was all my decision. I felt powerful."

"Oh, this is more than I'd hoped for. Mercer's not only lovely but a generous lover. So there will be a next time. How could there not when you make a simple kiss sound so glorious?"

Camille twisted her hands together in her lap. Dejected. Guilt-ridden. Ashamed. "No. The war hero doesn't want to cuckold Ridley, can you believe it? I suppose I was willing to, ye of little moral fiber. My one chance to experience passion before marriage to a man I feel no passion for, and Mercer's ruining it with his bloody *principles*." She said the last in the same tone as she'd say chamber pot. "In any case, he doesn't know what he wants. It was a kiss to kill, true, but nothing more. I stunned him, I stunned myself, but he still ran off with his tail between his legs. Champion sprinter, our devilish duke."

"So, only a kiss." Bel gave her pearls a good spin. "The killing kind, which must be the best."

Camille made a mark in the air. "Correct."

"With no proposal attached to it."

Another mark. "Correct."

"Then you'll simply have to compromise *him*. While we let him think it's his decision, since he's wavering. You'll force his hand in ways tried and true. Foolproof, feminine chicanery. We only have to devise a plan."

"Sounds like a devious trick to play on a family friend."

"I was compromised by multiple wonderful men in my youth, Camille. I highly recommend it. It's time men got theirs."

Countess Milburn chose this moment to stagger into the library, her ivory-tipped cane in hand. When it got later in the day, her hip tended to lock up, and she wouldn't dare use it if men were present. "He left, did he? Ruins my plans, right down the drain with the filthy bathwater."

Camille groaned low in her throat.

Bel gave her pearls an additional rattling shake. "Ridley had to get back to his mother. You know the dowager viscountess doesn't like to be alone in the Mayfair residence. As dangerous as a rookery to her mind. Evidently, a thousand servants aren't enough to comfort her."

The countess's limping shuffle sounded as she crossed the room, then Camille heard the decanter clink. So they were all going to get foxed this evening. "I don't care an owl's hoot about Ridley! My grand celebration just lost all significance. Imagine, a duke at the Milburn winter ball for the first time since Parnell attended in 1801. And he was nothing to look at, nothing like *this* one. Mercer's attendance would have hit the gossip sheets, posthaste. Everyone knows he's kept a low profile since blasted Waterloo. The rumor is, he's not even keeping a mistress. The opera singer was years ago, wasn't she, before he left?"

"Actress," Camille murmured.

"Well, no matter, because she's out of the picture. My ball could have served as his reintroduction to society. A chance to snatch up a wildly available man, if only for one night. I have a footman oil all the parlor and sitting room locks before a gathering. Incredibly well-maintained should a couple want to utilize the space for fifteen minutes or so. I don't mind innuendo but don't want an outright scandal occurring on the premises." She thumped her cane on the floor, three hard blows. "Behind bolted doors is best for all."

"Adelia," Bel gasped, "not in front of an unmarried girl if you please."

Camille opened her eyes to find the countess's belligerent gaze fixed on her. "Balderdash. She's no girl. Do you see the way she looks at him, like icing atop a biscuit. And don't go suggesting I'm talking about Ridley! If Mercer ran away with that level of heat licking his skin, my ball is doomed."

"I don't look at him like icing atop anything," Camille whispered from her slump on the settee, though she feared this was exactly how she'd looked at Tristan and always had. She palmed her aching chest, wishing to disappear from the room and this horrid conversation. "I don't even like him." *Although he kisses like a dream*, she thought somewhat distractedly, brandy a lingering influence.

"Like it or not, someday he has to marry and put an heir in place. I mentioned there would be several eligible young ladies in attendance." The countess threw herself into the chair closest to the fire, hooked her cane on the arm, and drank half her brandy in one gulp. "Not all horse-faced misses, either. Lady Monterey has promised to attend. And the Wellesley chit, she's quite nice to gaze upon. If only she wouldn't speak. Find a wife, find a mistress, up to you, I told him. I left it open, after alluding to my pristine locks. Always good to let the randy ones know in advance, is my policy."

Bel slapped her glass to the table. "Well, that settles it. He'll never come."

"Unless…" Adelia Rothingham-Wicket, Countess Milburn, once the loveliest creature to roam London, shot a sly look Camille's way. "Unless he has a reason to think he should."

Bel scooted forward on the settee, her knees popping. "I love it when you get that Machiavellian tone."

"Servants talk and men like competition," Adelia murmured into her glass. "I witnessed Mercer giving out his own share of piquant looks during our outing today, which is why my hip is acting up. The jaunt across an icy field, not adoring attention from a duke. Who needs a tree *inside* the house? Hope the blessed thing doesn't catch fire and burn you up in your sleep." She sucked on her teeth and nodded, agreeing with her unspoken suggestion. "What if a certain bit of gossip, another man interested in Lady Camille, for instance, a rival laudable enough to get Mercer's blood flowing, reached Tierney Hall's lower staff? They chatter the most. It wouldn't take much scheming for this tidbit to make it to Mercer's valet. He's had the same one, that old crone Oswald, since his youth. If the man has any inkling his duke is interested in someone, even if he doesn't want to be, this could work. And I get the finest winter ball since '01."

Camille lifted her head, unease racing through her as her aunt and the countess exchanged glowing looks. "Why would I agree to this?"

Adelia rolled her eyes and huffed out a savage breath. "Must we do all the work here? Because you want him."

"I don't want him."

"I'll try again. Because you want to know if he wants *you*. If he does, you can decide what to do with him."

Camille paused, alcohol swimming through her mind and muddling her thoughts. Did he want her? He'd admitted his attraction, but the Duke of Mercer had been attracted to many women if one believed the broadsheets Countess Milburn valued so much.

Unaccountably, spitefully, Camille admitted she wanted Tristan to want her so much it decimated him, as her adoration for him had always decimated her. Turnabout was fair play, after all. "I have Ridley," she finally said in a pained tone speaking little of being *glad* she had him or this wanting a duke to want her badly business.

"Posh, that's nothing to boast about. But the Duke of Mercer..." The countess sent a defiant glance over the rim of her glass. "If you're so prideful about your prior infatuation, which everyone in England is aware of and which you could take pitying advantage of, well then, we'll make him come to you. You're lovely, and he's noticed. It won't be hard."

Camille slid low on the settee, closing her eyes and praying for sleep to take her. "He won't agree to it. He won't come. You've seen the last of the man for months, years even."

Countess Milburn sniggered and her aunt, after one delicate breath of silence, joined in. Camille listened to them giggle and whisper and plot until slumber and a liberal dose of brandy claimed her.

CHAPTER 4

Where a waltz does the talking.

Tristan stood in a shadowy corner of the terrace, his back pressed to a snow-dusted windowpane, and gave the assemblage flowing into Countess Milburn's ancestral castle a bored glance—should anyone have sussed out his hiding place and taken leave to note his expression. He took an appreciative sip from his flask and slipped it back in his waistcoat pocket, wondering what the everlasting hell he was doing here.

Attending a winter ball in the Yorkshire countryside, that's what.

A decision made *after* his valet, the long-suffering Oswald, told him a juicy snippet he didn't wish to hear. When Tristan hated balls. Hated dancing, although he was quite good at it. Hated gossip and innuendo and answering questions about Waterloo and where he'd been disappearing to since he returned—*on darkened terraces, don't you know.* He wasn't charming anymore. Wasn't fit for his title, though he wanted it. Or wanted Tierney Hall, to be precise. He loved it more than any property he owned, and he owned five. His parents had routinely sent him to Yorkshire with his tutor and valet in tow, the servants stepping in where his family faltered. He hadn't wanted them to come with him. Not after he realized they weren't a real family.

Here, he'd always felt at home. At peace.

Turning, he took the stairs leading to the side garden, drawing a breath of air that frosted his lungs on contact. There would be a servant's entrance somewhere along the side of the house, near the kitchens, and he meant to use it. He'd show his face at this event, but he wasn't going through a bloody receiving line.

Not even for the chance to touch her again.

Ridley was temporarily out of the picture, but a handsome young marquess of some notoriety was interested in Camille and taking advantage of her betrothed's absence this very night. Which shouldn't have mattered one whit to Tristan, but here he was, tromping through ankle-deep slush, his Hessians, when no one wore boots to a ball, filthy, his breeches damp, his skin chilled. He was wounded, in soul if not body, the worst man for her should he have considered offering for her himself, which was *not* the plan. There was no room in his life for eyes the color of spring rain and kisses that made him forget what year it was.

Cunning looks and witty rejoinders and a sharp pinch of attraction he didn't remember feeling before.

He would act the protector, stepping in for her brother, Edward, since she and her aunt seemed unable to locate a good man between them.

With a weak curse, Tristan halted at the first service door he came to. What would Camille Bellington—female botanist and entrepreneur—think if he told her he'd spent the last forty-eight hours dodging memories of her fingers tangled in his hair, her lips molded to his, her breath, light and effervescent, sliding down his throat to dent his heart?

Dodging what he'd like to do if he got his hands on her.

Not exactly brotherly affection.

She'd be pleased; she wanted him to pay for not loving her back when it had been an impossibility.

Now, he was interested. And she was unavailable.

"Shit," he said and shoved the door open with his shoulder, music from the ballroom enveloping him like a hug. Ditching his coat and hat in a chair in the deserted hallway, he followed the sound of the orchestra, ignoring the startled looks of the kitchen staff as he muscled his way through them. The aroma was redolent of snug nights by the hearth, holidays, *family*.

Nothing he'd ever known.

As he took the stairs opposite the manor's main entrance down to the ballroom two at a time, Tristan gave the ache in his chest a hard rub. *What silliness was this?* He'd never been sentimental, never longed for children. Or a wife.

Tea and crumpets over *The Times*.

Pausing at the edge of the ballroom floor, couples engaged in a quadrille flitting in and out of his vision, he gathered his life was changing.

A rupture, a separation of the old from the new.

Because it was the way things were going, Camille stepped into view at the opposite end of the dancefloor, moving in and out of the rectangularly-patterned set with ease. Her hair breathing in candlelight from the many chandeliers and releasing it in a ginger burst. Perching against a marble column, Tristan appropriated a flute from the liveried footman and sipped champagne while he watched.

No patched gown this evening; no dirty-kneed termagant anywhere in sight.

She was magnificent. The loveliest woman in the room.

If Countess Milburn and Lady Fontaine were dangling Camille in front of him, which he'd considered might be happening, it was working.

His blood was pulsing with the longing to touch her again.

Sink his fingers in her auburn tresses and capture her lips beneath his. And be prepared for the implosion this time. Slide that exquisite gown—somewhere, depending upon one's opinion, between green and blue—right off her slender body and show her what it was to worship.

Tristan reined in his fascination and gazed about the room as if he cared who else was in it. A crowd had gathered, not too close, mind you, his temperament was suspect, but close enough.

Because he was part of the entertainment.

Who better to liven up a ball than a reluctant, battle-weary duke?

The final notes of the song sounded, and couples dipped into neat curtsies at the quadrille's close. When the musicians broke into the Sussex Waltz, Tristan made his decision. By God, he wasn't watching her waltz with another man, the bawdiest activity one was allowed to perform in public, while he felt this combustive. Over *her*. "Hold this for me, will you?" he asked and shoved his flute at an unimaginative baron he'd met years ago at an unimaginative musicale.

He was across the floor before Camille had a chance to catch her breath and locate her next partner. "Mine, I believe," he said, coming up behind her, a spot of treachery he could live with. "Lucky you, because I'm staggeringly good at the waltz, risqué though it may be." Lowering his voice, he closed his fingers about hers. "No dance requires the level of touching this one does. Be prepared, Princess, for the spin of your life."

"You arrogant oaf," she muttered as he tucked her into place. "Your name isn't on my card this round, and you know it."

He counted off the rhythm, then led her into the dance, sweeping her through the first rotation effortlessly. For a tall woman, she was light as a proverbial feather, following his charge without objection, their bodies in picture-perfect alignment. It made downright *shocking* images flood his mind. He shook his head and found the wit to respond. "You dare to defy a duke?"

"Oh, my, no. I would never." She dipped her chin and batted her lashes, demure as a tigress.

His laughter had her looking up and into his face with an expression of pure astonishment, honesty, and *avarice*.

His breath caught as the world fell away.

Candlelight shimmered off the unpredictable eyes fixed on him—dark as bluebells this evening—as he maneuvered their owner through a turn, swirling her around the parquet floor as if they'd been born to dance here, on this night, together. Hunger for her, and only her, burned a trail from his brain to his cock. "Your gown is the same color as your eyes. In reality, they're a different shade every time I look at them. I admit to being spellbound in anticipation of what I may receive."

Camille's step didn't waver as her lips pressed tight. In annoyance or amusement, he couldn't tell. "Silliness, this talk. After you forced me into this, you should behave yourself."

"My attraction to you is silly?" His eyebrow rose, just the one, a trick women usually liked. "And when have you known me to behave myself?"

"This discussion is silly," she said, her tone severe. "And, good point."

Definitely annoyed, he decided. "Are you surprised to see

me, at least? I don't usually attend these things, you know. Only Almack's is worse."

"Countess Milburn is dizzy with delight, I'm sure. The best winter ball since 1801."

His fingers tightened around hers as visions of them tumbling across his bed raced through his mind. Her scent, peony and orange blossoms, rolled over him like a wave and took him under. "Are you dizzy with delight, Princess? And if not, how can I get you to be?"

He didn't know why he asked this when he was running full-speed away from her.

Or trying to. And failing.

While he pondered this dilemma, managing his enchanting botanist through another elegant rotation, somewhere behind him, a glass hit the floor and exploded with a bang. To Tristan's unmitigated mortification, the sound plunged him into the anarchy of a rain-soaked field in Belgium, the chalky scent of death crushing, the bitter taste of fear choking.

All at once, he was at war, and the memories were swallowing him whole.

"*Tristan.*" Camille yanked his sleeve—and this was when he apprehended he'd brought them to a standstill in the middle of the ballroom, puzzled couples darting around them.

She repeated his name, more urgently this time.

He gazed at her and blinked slowly. "I'm fine," he whispered when he was reasonably sure he wasn't. And as he'd been trying to tell her, might never be again.

Camille grasped his forearm and smiled, fanning her face like she'd gotten warm and needed a reprieve. Nodding at anyone who looked their way, she gestured to the refreshment table as if they'd discussed food and drink as a remedy. She was quick, this woman, razor-sharp. She would have made a fine soldier. Tristan wanted to tell her this, she'd have liked it, he imagined, but he had to focus or anxiety would triumph and completely ruin the evening.

As it was, he wasn't going to sleep for days.

Camille grabbed a glass from a passing footman and shoved it in his hand. "Drink, Tris. Your skin has gone the color of daisy petals."

He drained the glass, the wine stinging the back of his throat but doing little to mist his mind. "Is that good?"

She shook her head, her gaze probing as she searched his face. "I don't think so."

"I may need a moment," he admitted when he recognized how badly his hands were shaking. "Can you make excuses for me? A loose button, a sudden headache?"

"The countess has a wide variety of sitting rooms with doors that lock. Find one."

Tristan laughed, although blackness was edging his vision, and panic was beginning to swell. "Yes, she mentioned those. In excellent working order should I have the urge to ravish anyone this evening."

Camille flushed, her gaze dropping to her slippers.

Damned if they weren't in trouble, both of them, he thought desperately.

After an awkward silence, she took his glass and gestured with it to a hallway leading off the ballroom. "I'll render apologies should the countess want to know where you've run off to. Should I keep a list of the eligible ladies who stop by hoping to be ravished?"

"Naturally." He turned, heading toward a discreet salon of his choice. "That reminds me," he said and glanced over his shoulder, "apparently a handsome marquess is trying to run you to ground now that Ridley's gone off to be with his mommy. I think I was summoned to intervene. Hold my place, should this occur. I'll regain my ducal fighting stance swiftly, I promise."

Then he stumbled from the ballroom before he let society see what war did to a man.

Throughout a cotillion and a Scotch reel, Camille worried about the way color had bled from Tristan's cheeks. As she tried to imagine what dread like that must *feel* like, she stepped on Lord Heming's toes and got lost during her conversation with Baron Birmingham. When Viscount Arnold approached for his selection, she claimed to have a torn hem and took herself off to find Tristan.

This worrying without action would not do.

She located him in the fourth room she tried.

He didn't turn from his study of the woodlands surrounding the countess's estate, simply stood quietly before the window sipping from a glass. He looked lonely. On an island he didn't want anyone else to reach, the glow from a candelabra turning the tips of his hair gold and gilding his skin. Camille turned the key in the lock, and the dull clink echoed through the room.

"They're like nightmares while I'm awake. I don't know why, but startling sounds bring them to the forefront of my mind. Like they're close, shallowly buried and easy to retrieve." He braced his hand on the window ledge and gazed into the snowy night. "Only needing a jolt to reveal them. Then I'm tossed into the pit."

Skirting the desk he stood behind, she settled in beside him, shoulders touching, and took his glass. Gin. It burned as it went down, and she coughed.

"Easy," Tristan said without looking at her, a hint of a smile in his voice.

She pushed the glass back in his hand, a hand that no longer shook, she noted. "I walked in on Lady Pierce-Nesmith two doors down on her knees before a man, a man most definitely *not* Lord Pierce-Nesmith. It was, if nothing else, enlightening."

Tristan turned to her with a sputtered laugh. "You're kidding."

Camille grimaced, recalling what she'd seen in the two-second flash. "I wish I were."

"Don't they know about the famous Milburn locks?" He tipped his glass her way. "Which I noticed you wisely employed."

Stepping back, she rested her bottom on the desk. Tristan had located a study of some sort to hide in. Bookcases, armchairs, dark corners, dust. Nothing romantic about it. A room for reflection, not seduction. "Has this happened before?"

He flicked his fingers, dismissing the question. "No matter. But I think it proves a fine point, in light of our recent...transactions. Why I can't marry. Why I can't live with anyone. Sleep through the night with anyone. You think this was dreadful, the dreams are worse. The dreams are horrendous." When she started to speak, he held her off with a stern look. "Not right now, Princess. Maybe not ever. You see, old Ridley is right about one thing, aside from his fascination with you. I'm no longer fit for society. I no longer belong."

Camille gazed at his pensive silhouette, her heart seizing, wondering why she had to love such a complicated man. Because she did love him, she always had, and her continued feelings were a disaster in the making. Desire pulsed through her as she stood there, his scent—the faintest hint of smoke and sandalwood—drifting to her, the heat from his body crossing the short distance separating them and cloaking her like a woolen shawl. She recognized what she wanted. His hands on her body, his teeth nipping her skin, his lips claiming hers. She didn't want this from Ridley, and she never would.

She'd not experienced true passion and had no idea how to make it happen, but she knew in her soul what she felt.

"What can I do to erase those memories?" she asked, thrilled by her daring but frightened by her absolute lack of knowledge.

He slowly lifted his head, his eyes as dark as baize in the candlelight. "Best not ask during a weak moment, because I'm not sure I can deny myself." But defying himself, he stepped close, threaded his fingers through her hair, scattering pins as he tilted her head high. "If you only understood where this will go if I allow it. If I allow you to take me there."

She gasped, her lids fluttering as his nails scored her scalp, a gentle abrasion that sent longing spiraling between her thighs, hardening her nipples to fine points beneath her shift.

"You smell like summer," he murmured, his breath brushing her cheek. "Like cool ponds and wheat fields, like passion and promise and *want*. The way the world was before I witnessed another side. The world I wish I could step back into. After a kiss that killed, is there more?" His lips brushed her jaw, the side of her mouth, lingering, teasing. "I think we're both wondering."

Grasping her waist, he set her fully on the desk, nudged her knees apart, and stepped in until their hips bumped. She sighed, her gaze dropping. Beneath his buckskin close, his rigid length tented his breeches. Long and hard and beautiful.

A burst of feminine power lit her from within. To have

his body react to her in this way seemed no less than a miracle.

Astounded, she looked up at him in wonder.

In the milky candlelight, his face took on a thunderous cast. "You should be frightened, Camille. We aren't playing; we're no longer children." He nodded to the door, a tight breath racing from his lips. "Locked in, I could seduce you, here, now. Tangle us both up in need, toss every plan you've made for yourself in the hearth, and turn your future to ashes. It's happened a thousand times in a thousand parlors with a thousand people who later wished it hadn't." He exhaled again, irritated and torn. "Why aren't you letting me do the right thing?"

"I don't know," she whispered and set her lips to his, knowing not what to do, only knowing she had to touch him.

Sliding one hand behind her neck, he released a primal sound and lifted her off the desk and into him. His lips moved over hers, again and again, until he sighed in frustration. Cradling her jaw, he tilted her head, the slight adjustment putting them in flawless alignment—and sending the kiss rocketing into an alternate universe.

There could be no two people who'd fit together more magically.

She wanted to learn, wanted to bring him to his knees, the girl who'd fought for his attention still very much a part of her. So she followed his every move, shyly touched her tongue to his, swirled it in the rhythm he was echoing below her waist, pressing the tantalizing part of himself, even harder than when they'd started, into her most secret of places. She matched him measure for measure, finally losing all reason, clutching his shoulders and kissing him back with nothing but a blind reach for *more*.

More contact. Deeper. Faster. *Harder*.

Perhaps she whispered her plea, because he was there.

Setting her gently back on the desk, yanking layers of clothing high, reaching through the slit in her drawers, and touching her as she'd touched herself in her darkened bedchamber, but on this night, knowing exactly, *exactly*, where to go when she'd fumbled.

He understood—and brought swift pleasure.

Their kiss was impossible to maintain with his fingers circling, pressing, fondling, lighting a fire inside her, making her vision blur and her breath shorten. Her head fell back on a husky moan as she scooted forward, begging without words. If he would just...

"This is what you're looking for, Princess," he whispered into her neck. Sucking her earlobe between his teeth, he slid a finger inside her, a delightful breach, a delicious surrender. "Don't think," he added breathlessly as he invaded her body with sure, flawless strokes. "This is what I'm giving you. You fought for it, now take it."

So she did.

Closed her eyes and let sensation override fear. Of losing her soul when he'd always owned her heart. Of recognizing no other man could touch her in this way, make her *want* in this way.

Greedy and desperate, she consumed.

The feel of his long body curled over hers, lips at her jaw, his hair, soft and silky, brushing her temple. Hand gripping the nape of her neck, holding her steady as he plundered. A ticking clock. The call of a raven outside the window. The faint murmur of the orchestra belowstairs. Overridden only by her raspy cries, sounds she was unable to contain or classify.

She would have been embarrassed if she'd been able to be anything but his.

The feeling started as a buzz in her head, a swirl of anticipation in her belly. Her fingers tingled, her thighs clenched.

"That's it," he murmured and slowed his rhythm. His hand went to cradle her jaw, tipping her head back. "Open your eyes. My gift, what I'm taking, is to witness what color yours turn when you come."

She followed his command, for once willing to, and found his gaze devouring her, his expression frenzied. He shifted his arm, swept his thumb over the peaked nub at the juncture of her core. Once, twice. Her lids fluttered as she ceded to his caress. "*No*, keep them open. Look at me when you crest." He swallowed, his throat clicking. "*Please*," he begged when she guessed he'd never begged for anything in his life.

It was too much. His voice, his touch.

What he was doing to her was too much.

She fell against him, pressed her cry of pleasure into his shoulder, her shudders into his chest. He brought her close, kissed her brow, her cheek, murmured tender, meaningless words in her ear.

For a long instant, he continued to touch her, drawing bliss from her body as he would water from a well until she had to push him away. Until she was bone-dry. "No more...I can't."

Stepping back, he straightened her skirts, gathered her hairpins from the desk. All with his breath shooting from his lips, his breeches still deliciously tented, his hands trembling. Finally, with a sigh, he closed them into fists and came to a full stop.

"You," Camille whispered in sudden realization. He was still in a state of need. Surely, she could deliver pleasure if he told her what to do.

Imagining such intimacy sent a dizzying burst through her. She guessed she'd be good at it if she tried. "Tell me what to do," she said and reached for him.

Swearing, Tristan stumbled back, her hairpins scattering across the rug. "That's not happening. Apologies for being vulgar, but if you touch me"—he grazed the heel of his hand down his shaft, unleashing the wild desire simmering beneath her skin—"I'll spill like a schoolboy and have a mess in my trousers *and* my head. Thank you, but I can take care of this later. I'm quite proficient, as most men are. The knotty business in my brain may take longer."

"*I* want to take care of you. Here, now." She sounded petulant, like the girl who'd annoyed him over the years when men didn't usually seek out bothersome lovers.

He searched, found his glass on the window ledge and drained it. "Yes, that's apparent." Glancing over his shoulder, his eyes flashed in the chalky moonlight, the color of the first grass of spring. "It's the tastiest offer I've had in my life. I want to say yes to anything you suggest we try, you have no idea how desperately, but I'm not going to."

Scrambling off the desk, she came up behind him. "Why not? After, after..." She gestured to herself, an inclusive movement, not sure how to vocalize what he'd done to her. "We *know* each other now."

He hung his head and laughed, the sound filling the room with as much heat as a raging hearthfire. By the time he swiveled to face her, she was aroused and angry, vexed beyond belief after such unmitigated pleasure.

Perching on the ledge, he dangled the empty glass between his spread legs, likely to hide the situation beneath his trouser close, the cad. "We don't *know* each other in that way. This, and the damned kiss that started it, only prove how well we work together. Chemistry. We have it. In spades." He glanced down, kicked his boots around, then looked back at her. "I can see from the obstinate look on your face you don't believe me." Shrugging, his lips canted in a regrettable half-smile. "Do you know what I was thinking while I had my finger deep inside you? I was imagining the ways I could take you. Bent over the desk, filling you from behind. With my cock, not my finger, if I may be so bold. Dragging you to the floor and taking your hard nipples between my teeth as I discover what makes you forget yourself even more than you just did. Dropping to my knees and pleasuring you that way. My *favorite* way." He tapped his glass against his knee with a lost look. "You think my hand is wondrous? My lips are *destructive*."

His portrayal certainly didn't match how ladies of the *ton* described sexual congress in heated whispers.

She had much, so much, to learn.

"I thought about putting my mouth on you, too," she murmured, dazed by his speech and the images storming her mind.

"Go back to the ball, Princess," he said between clenched teeth. "Before you push my unexpected streak of honor too far. Because I'm not going to do anything else I lie away at night hating myself for." He tipped the glass her way. "Even for you."

Shaken, she stalked to the door, flipped the lock with a curse she hoped he was surprised she knew. "I'm not sorry," she said without looking at him. "I'm not going to be one of the thousand people in a thousand parlors who wish they hadn't."

She was in the hallway, five steps from the room, when she heard crystal shatter against the wall.

CHAPTER 5

Where there is salvation in false starts.

The plums were a surprise, Camille concluded, cupping her hand around a fruit and pulling it loose. She'd nursed the tree through the fall and winter, checked water levels daily, and experimented with different fertilizers. But she hadn't expected it to bud. And in the middle of winter, no less. The humid greenhouse climate the only reason it had. The poor thing didn't realize it was December. In Yorkshire.

This tree was going to be the making of her as an amateur botanist. It would be the reason the society in London finally agreed to speak to a female. The gentlemen on the committee had no idea a new variety of plum had been located in Sussex.

She was going to enjoy telling them.

"Camille Elise, I can't believe you're awake after such a long night." Her aunt entered the conservatory with a clatter, the door slamming behind her. She patted her head and smiled crookedly, carefully avoiding ceramic pots and bags of soil on her way to her niece. "Megrims, you know. Too much wine, too much dancing." Giggling, she made a prancing swirl down the center aisle. "But it was such fun. The countess does throw a marvelous bash! Definitely her best in years. Mercer made the evening, showing up as he did. Though he didn't stay long. But one cannot argue with success. You shared a waltz, and the *ton* is humming. Everyone's so thrilled he's back."

Camille dropped a plum in the straw basket sitting at her feet. "I'll be sure to tell him."

Her aunt stumbled and righted herself against the wooden bench housing a variety of garden tools. "What did you say? Something about Mercer?" She banged her ear with the heel of her hand. "You caught me on the bad side. That horrendous cold three years ago. I can't hear the same out of it. Distressing, but what can one do? The local sawbones didn't help one whit. Hot oil drops, posh!"

Camille looped the basket over her forearm and settled a linen napkin atop the bounty inside. "I'm jilting Ridley, Bel. I sent a letter in this morning's post. A very humble, apologetic message, taking all manner of responsibility for the decision." She glanced at her aunt, then away, through the wall of windows. The sky was a clear, brilliant blue. As sure as her decision. "But it's jilting just the same."

Bel puffed out her cheeks and released a gusty breath. "Not especially nice to announce this right before Christmas. His mother will be distraught, poor thing. You'll be on her list, and I've heard she has a long one. Expect to be cut dead when you see her, for the rest of her life. The dowager viscountess never forgets or forgives."

"Better that than marrying her son when I don't love him."

Picking a splinter of wood loose from the bench, Bel twirled it between her fingers. "No one believed it was love, darling."

Camille stepped close and grasped her aunt's hand. Tears pricked her lids, and she blinked them back. "I can't save Longleat. Not by marrying a man I don't want, who doesn't, if he considers it carefully, want me. I'm too independent, too stubborn, and I would have made Ridley miserable. I thought I could do it, marry him to save us. But I find, after... well, I find I cannot. Please forgive me."

Bel drew her into her arms, and love flooded Camille's heart. "Oh, my lovely girl, you have nothing to apologize for. We'll find a way to save the estate, never you fear. If you marry Mercer—"

Camille pushed from her hold, the basket banging her hip. "Tristan and I aren't going to be together. He feels he can't marry, and I won't accept anyone else."

Bel frowned in confusion and nodded to the basket. "But you're picking fruit for him!"

"He liked the plums. I'm going to give them to him before I seduce him."

Fanning her cheeks, Bel looked around for a place to sit. "I feel faint. Elated but faint."

Camille grabbed a wooden bucket and flipped it over, settling her aunt atop it and crouching beside her.

"Dear me," Bel said and dropped her head to her hands, her body wobbling with the rock of her seat. "Seduce him, you said?"

Sitting back on her heels, Camille searched for a way to explain. She understood her rationale but didn't expect anyone else to. "If I'm not to marry, what's the harm in letting myself experience passion? With someone I'm attracted to. Someone kind. Someone I *trust*."

"A gorgeous duke we suspect is excellent in bed," Bel said from between her fingers. "Don't leave out the best part."

"Are you going to try and stop me?"

Bel knocked her bonnet aside and gazed from beneath the twisted brim. "Why would I when I agree?"

Camille blinked. "You do?"

She cupped her niece's cheek, her eyes full of affection and fond memories. "You could have married Ridley and been content, I suppose. If you didn't know passion existed. I'm guessing something happened with Mercer at the ball, and now you do. I could have done the same, married for convenience, for money, a business arrangement beneficial to both parties. But there was a man, long ago, a baronet without a penny to his name. Not a farthing. My family wouldn't allow it, of course, and I was too young to know to fight for him. But he…" She sighed and laughed, her gaze sliding to her slippers. "He ruined me for marriage. After his kiss, his touch, I could accept no other as my husband. Better this"—she indicated her life in one broad gesture—"than that. I'm content. I made the right choice."

"He's going to break my heart," Camille whispered, closing her eyes at the thought of it.

"Oh, darling." Bel bussed her cheek. "I think it's more likely you'll break his."

#

Tristan pictured the gentle curve of Camille's breast for the fourth time in minutes and smashed his thumb with the hammer. Hissing an oath, he stepped back from the pile of decaying boards he'd stripped from the hunting lodge's wall and shook his throbbing hand. His childhood hideaway, he'd come here when his parents began hurling insults and dishes, when he was lonely or scared or bored. It had been his castle. Over the years, his father had allowed the dwelling to slide into a deplorable state along with the rest of the estate.

Tristan had a team of workers doing repairs at Tierney Hall, but here, in this most personal of places, he wanted the work to be his and his alone.

He wanted to propel himself into a state of exhaustion as he restored his ancestral home, fatigue leaving no room for dreams of war or women.

He wanted to forget about her, the girl who'd tried to pet a swan, the woman who'd waltzed with him beneath the glow of a thousand candles.

The woman he'd taken in his arms and whispered his secrets to.

She made him want to share himself.

His past, his future.

Before, he'd believed he was broken. Now, he suspected he was only wounded. Healing slowly, but *healing*. Even the little he'd told her about Waterloo had released the pressure in his chest like he'd jammed a nail in a cask and let the contents trickle out. Miraculous, that reckoning, a furious flood of sunshine after two years of gloom.

Tristan dropped to his haunches to trace his finger along a split in the rotted walnut paneling, his taut exhalation fogging the morning air. Somehow, his childhood nemesis, the girl he'd fondly considered a bothersome nuisance, was helping him find his way.

He hadn't anticipated falling in love, which he believed might be happening. Uncertainty, confounding joy. Unadulterated distress. The first person he hadn't been able to shove from his mind no matter how hard he tried to.

Obsession. Fascination. Bewilderment.

Sounded like love to him.

Which left two choices. Either fight for her—or let Ridley win. Tristan brought the hammer down on a rotted board at the thought.

While he kneeled there, his mind in turmoil, the faint

scent of orange blossoms whispered through his senses, and he turned to find Camille standing in the doorway, basket in hand, sunlight oozing around her, the certainty of his feelings confirmed by the answering flicker of happiness lighting his soul.

He stared, unable to find a witty retort. Compose a plea, a confession, an avowal. Make light of an impossible situation with a smile, laugh, or wink. He was undone by her beauty, by the bashful look on her face. By the knowledge she'd loved him when he wasn't lovable, that she'd cared and, somehow, miraculously, hadn't gotten over it.

Her eyes swept his body, her cheeks flushing, and he recalled his lack of proper clothing. Shirtsleeves rolled to the elbow, faded trousers ripped at the knee and thigh, braces hanging limply at his hip. "I jilted Ridley," she murmured when her gaze crawled back to his, so quietly he struggled to hear the admission.

But he did—and he was on his feet and across the room, pressing her against the doorjamb before either of them took another breath. Her basket slipped from her hand, plums bouncing along the scuffed planks.

"I know you can't, that we won't—"

"*Don't*," he said, his mind and heart tied in a feverish knot. "Just let me touch you with no one between us."

She brought her hand to his chest. *Don't leave*, he thought and pressed his lips to her hair. The silken strands smelled of pine and nutmeg, the kitchens and her conservatory, and he drew deeply, feeling grounded, feeling like he was home for the first time in forever.

"I'm not leaving," she whispered and bounced to her toes, pressing her lips to his in an eager, artless move that pocketed what remained of his heart until she owned it all.

Grasping her shoulders, he moved her away from the door, slamming it shut with his boot. Then he dove in, meeting her hungry kiss with one providing what he'd long denied giving. Himself, love, forgiveness.

Everything.

He slowed, one hand sliding to her hip, the other rising to cradle the nape of her neck, taking each languid beat of time to show her. How they fit, how they belonged together. His tongue caressing hers, swirling, engaging, as she mirrored his efforts, turning the tables until she taught, and he learned. What she liked, what she craved, what made her release those helpless, panting breaths against his lips. Mouths molded, blood racing, hearts thumping.

Hand moving to her lower back, he brought her in, hips pressed, his body straining for release.

Want, need, *yearning.*

She whimpered and wiggled from his grasp, brought her hands to his shirt and fumbled with the bone buttons. "Off."

He smiled and tipped her head high, her eyes meeting his. "I can't promise to make it last, not the first time. Not when I want you this badly. I'll be better after. It's been…it's been a long time, Princess. It's been forever." Swallowing hard, he pressed an impatient kiss to her brow. "Tell me you're sure. I need to know you're sure."

She mouthed the words—*first, after*—with curiosity in her eyes, and his heart bottomed out. She hadn't known…? Had believed touching her once would be enough?

Grabbing her hand, he pulled her down the short hallway and into the lodge's lone bedroom. A fire blazed in the hearth, a breeze from the window he'd cracked to allow winter entry sending the flames dancing. He'd been sleeping here, not the main house. Which was evident from the linen shirt tossed across the armchair, the book of Shelley's poems on the bedside table, his razor and strap sitting atop the nicked armoire. His ledgers and correspondence scattered over a desk he'd appropriated from storage.

Brushing past him, she walked to the center of the room and turned in a tight circle, taking it in. His private space. His private life. "So, this is where the duke lives."

He waited for her gaze to make it back to his. Her eyes were magnificent in the muted light, as blue-green as the lake on the western edge of his estate. "This is where Tristan lives. The duke you speak of"—he shrugged, not able to answer—"I don't know him well. Maybe someday, I will." He moved a step closer. "But know this. I want you here. I want *us* here. More than you can imagine. And this is a place I've never brought another living soul."

She crossed to him and wordlessly started unbuttoning his shirt. When he took a stuttered inhalation as her fingers brushed his chest, she glanced at him through long, dark lashes. "I propose we get the first time out of the way since you made the second sound so thrilling. Apologies for being forward."

"I like it," he whispered and allowed her touch, knowing he was giving her even more of himself than she imagined. When she saw…

As his shirt fluttered to the floor, her soft gasp lit the air. Witnessing the mottled scar on his shoulder for the first time, she didn't react as expected. She didn't ask him to share a memory he wasn't sure he could share yet. She simply pressed her lips to a wound that had almost killed him on a somber battlefield, healing him as the calvary's surgeon hadn't.

When she began to shadow the trail of hair arrowing down his chest and into his waistband, his lips seized hers, and he backed her toward the bed. His cock couldn't take direct contact, not if he wanted to make it inside her without shattering.

With a wicked smile, he wrapped her hands around the bedpost and stepped behind her. "Hold on, Princess. As hard as you need to." Then he began to undress her—ties, buttons, hook and thread loops—deliberately relaxed, caressing each bit of skin he exposed to his hungry gaze. A light dusting of freckles on her shoulder, a pale scar on her lower back. Slim hips, firm thighs, delicate ankles. Leaving no part of her untouched, he recognized he was unjustly seducing her, kissing, nibbling, stroking, retreating, leaving her naked, gasping, aroused.

When she released a pointed growl of impatience, he kicked aside her puddle of clothing and rose to his feet. "I'm being unfair," he murmured and began to slide her hairpins free. Leaning in, he brushed his lips along the delicate curve from her shoulder to the nape of her neck. "Inequitable attention."

"You're a bounder," she sighed, her cheek pressed to the bedpost, her eyes closed, her skin moist, her breathing heavy.

"You're the loveliest thing I've ever seen, Camille Bellington. I want you to know that before I lose myself in you, when I'll be unable to string together a sentence, I fear." He drew his thumb down her spine, rolling over each pressure point with deliberate intensity. "Turn around."

"Take the trousers off. And the drawers. Every piece while I watch. To balance out the inequities, you see." Opening her eyes, she gazed at him over her shoulder. "Then, I'll do whatever you like."

His fingers fumbled with the buttons on his close, trying to hide his surprise that she was willing to play. He loved exploring, loved going off-script. But it wasn't customary. One had to be extremely comfortable to follow such impulses, and he wasn't sure he'd ever truly *been* comfortable with anyone.

Not completely. Not like this.

"Oh," she breathed when he finally stood before her,

unclothed, rigid, aching with need. She'd turned around, as promised, her gaze doing a painfully laborious study.

"You're killing me with that look, Princess."

She laughed, pressing back into the bedpost. "I'm sorry, but you're bloody beautiful, Tris. If those spitting cats had any idea you looked like *this* beneath your stylish layers, they'd break down your door."

He smiled sheepishly, embarrassed for the first time in memory. He was *not* the most beautiful person in the room. But a blush was lurking just beneath his skin and admitting this would unleash it.

With a knowing grin, she crooked her finger, beckoning. "Come here, Your Grace, and make it up to me for telling the world about my Serpentine battle with a swan."

#

Camille didn't know where she got the courage to laugh. To act like she had any idea what she was doing in this arena. To trade glib barbs with the handsomest man in England while he leisurely peeled off his clothing.

Now, Tristan Tierney, Duke of Mercer, naked as the day he was born, was pushing her back on his massive bed and crawling atop her. Breath short, color high, as if she'd shaken him as he'd shaken her.

Sucking her earlobe between his teeth, he settled with a groan between her thighs. "I'm too heavy."

He was. And it was *glorious*.

She wanted to chronicle this night, slap mental paint to canvas, but his hands were *everywhere*, making her lose sense and intellect. He hummed beneath his breath and slid his arm underneath her, lifting her against his turgid length. His lips capturing hers as he began to move, a surge and retreat she followed, skin to skin, going liquid at her core. He seemed to know what she needed, cupping her breast, sweeping his thumb over her nipple. Back and again, circling, leaving the nub peaked and throbbing.

Leaving her to do naught but plead for more.

Obeying, he broke the kiss and skimmed his way south, replacing his thumb with his lips. She arched off the bed at the feel of his teeth catching her nipple, the stubble on his jaw a luscious abrasion, her ragged moan frantic, her fingers sinking into his hair and guiding his movements.

"Your body is a treasure, Princess." He suckled the curve of her breast, his hand sliding over her stomach, her waist, her thigh. "And I'm going to worship at the altar."

His touch, when he slipped his fingers between her legs, was familiar. Like she'd known, without truly knowing, that he would be the man to introduce her to pleasure. He stroked, lightly, tenderly, warming her body and her mind. Returning to kiss her, his touch grew determined as he slid a long finger inside her and gave it a small twist…and then it was too much to document.

His weight atop her, his breath on her cheek, his tongue leading hers into a dance he echoed below her waist. The scent of them tangling with the scent of starched bedding and burning wood and winter frost. She wanted to touch, too, her hands on his shoulders, his chest, thumbing his nipple. He delighted in each caress, his groans mixing with hers until they couldn't be separated, those raw sounds of delight. Louder than the tick of the mantel clock, than winter's whisper shooting in the raised windowpane.

He stroked her once, the same place that had made her shatter the night of the ball, and the spiral began low in her belly. Pleading, she released a choking sound and lifted her hips.

"This?" he whispered against her lips, his voice frayed, and gave the tipped nub a harder caress.

She nodded, unable to speak. *Yes.*

He touched her more persistently until, her back arching off the mattress, she broke into a thousand pieces.

Then, he was there, murmuring soothing words and sliding inside her as tremors rocked her, his entry so gentle—and her body so open to him—she experienced only the slightest instant of pain. Dazed, she clutched his shoulders and lifted her hips, rising, bringing him deeper...deeper. The feeling of fullness and, *ah*, being transported to another world entirely was incredible.

"Cami," he murmured into her moist skin, the tension in his body proving he was as affected, as taken, as she was. "Slow down. I can't keep up, I can't think. I'm losing control."

Their pelvises bumped when he was fully entrenched, and she grasped his face between her palms, bringing his gaze to hers. His eyes were as green as a midnight forest, the dark pupils swallowing them whole. Sweat beaded his cheeks, his jaw, pooling in the hollow beneath his neck. She wanted to taste him, drink him in. Wreck him as he was wrecking her. "I don't want you in control. I want you feral, insatiable. *You*. Your body, your soul. Your mind can stay behind for now. Take me, I'm begging you," she said and dragged his lips to hers, whispering against them, "there's always the next time for control. The after, remember?"

Palming her thigh, he raised her leg high on his hip and settled, unbelievably, deeper inside her. Slow strokes progressed to swift, pounding ones, the joining of their bodies the only sound except for choked breaths and muffled moans. The bed began to rock and creak. Slick skin and grasping hands, a frantic joining of lips, tongues, teeth. She was a bird flying through the night, and he was her guide.

On a hard pulse of pleasure, she gasped and arched, losing her rhythm and the kiss, darkness edging her vision as a wave of ecstasy, more potent than any she'd experienced, caught her in its grip. Pressing her cheek to the mattress, she watched Tristan's hand twist in the counterpane until his knuckles whitened, and this exhibit of arousal pushed her over the edge.

"Thank God," he whispered into her shoulder as she convulsed around him, her cry ringing through the room. He held her close as she shuddered, then he followed seconds later, his arms tensing, his groan tortured, her name spilling from his lips the most erotic sound she'd ever heard.

To think she'd done this to him, left him panting, trembling...

For a long moment, they lay still, limbs tangled, skin slick, lungs churning.

When Camille was able to open her eyes, she found Tristan braced on his elbows, staring down at her with a look of bewilderment. "I just died and went to heaven," he rasped and rolled to his back, pulling her with him. She collapsed atop his chest, his heartbeat pounding beneath her ear, her own a dizzying rush through her veins. Head to toe, she was a quivering mass of nerve endings. And between her legs, a part of her body that would never be the same, oh, *my*...

"Tris, is it always—"

"*No*," he said, cutting off her question. He laughed weakly and tightened his arm around her, his rough kiss dusting the crown of her head. "Good God, no. If it were, people wouldn't leave the house. I've never experienced anything like this, Princess. Like *you*."

Camille wanted to ask more. How many positions were there? Did it sometimes last longer? When could he do it again? Because she could do it again, her body was ready. But the pang of jealousy constricting her chest meant her heart was not. *That damned actress*, she groused and blew a sigh across his collarbone. Fathoming that he'd experienced anything close to this with another woman sliced like a blade.

Pride and possession she had no right to feel battled inside her.

This was the danger, the risk, the trap.

Owning Tristan, even for one night, and losing him to fate, to life, was going to rip her apart. Her childhood obsession becoming her one, true love now seemed marginally hard to manage when she'd thought it would be easy to experience this and leave him to his life while continuing on with hers.

"What's the fit of pique?" he asked in a sleepy rumble. "Even in my near delirium, I can feel your mind churning."

She drew a circle around his nipple and watched it pebble, felt his body tense. "You promised two. Times. The after, remember?"

He mumbled a vague response.

She waited, the silence drawing out as she trailed her hand down his body. His sex was hardening when she wrapped her fingers around it. She'd not touched him there yet. Rigid, silky smooth, moist. *Wonderful.*

"You're insatiable, is that it?" His tone was light but filled with a breathless urgency that told her she was doing something right.

"Maybe," she returned and stroked, learning her way. Then his hand was there, guiding her, showing her what he liked.

She could, she reasoned, get used to this.

He groaned softly, deep in his throat. "I suppose I must stand by my promise." Sinking his fingers into her hair, he rolled, pressing her into the mattress and claiming her.

And she was lost.

CHAPTER 6

Where a discarded letter causes trouble.

Camille watched Tristan sleep as the moon crawled high in the sky, milky light flooding the bedchamber and bathing the world white. Midnight or just after, she'd guess. Sitting up, she stretched and shifted, feeling unfamiliar twinges in a well-loved body.

Love.

Gazing at him, she cataloged his every feature from head to toe, able to do so without his probing green eyes throwing her off-balance. He looked younger, long eyelashes dusting his cheek, slender lips slightly parted, innocent in a way he wasn't. Not anymore. She frowned and reached to trace the scar on his shoulder, then drew her hand back. He didn't sleep well. Nightmares, which he'd told her about in brief. So she wouldn't wake him. Not when they'd made love three times already, and he'd tumbled into sleep after the last with little more than a kiss and sigh. She giggled and pressed the back of her hand to her lips. *Three.* Who would have imagined it? Twice in Tristan's bed and once while standing, her legs wrapped around his hips, back pressed to the wall. So he'd been the only one on his feet.

Such a different feeling, that position, like he touched her in places he couldn't while lying down. He'd barely made it inside her before her release began to overtake her.

She dreamily shook her head, still dazed from their night together.

Drawing the wrinkled sheet to his chest, Camille crawled from the bed, snatched Tristan's shirt from the floor, and snaked her arms through the sleeves. Her stomach growled, and she remembered she hadn't had a bite to eat since breakfast. And it was freezing in the bedchamber. She'd round up whatever foodstuff was in the lodge, the plums she'd brought if nothing else, start a fire in the hearth…and tell him she loved him. Ask him, not beg, mind you, to consider giving them a chance. Despite his fears about the future, despite hers about losing her independence, *this*…she glanced back at her slumbering duke, this could very well be *something.*

Something magical, something extraordinary.

Something like love.

The wadded foolscap lying on the faded carpet caught her eye as she passed the desk. Glancing back, she noted Tristan's chest rising and falling in a fixed rhythm. Crouching, she smoothed the sheet flat with her hand. A nagging prick of guilt hit her, but she lifted the letter into the moonlight and read it anyway.

A before-unknown inheritance should arrive by Christmas. A deceased cousin of Lady Bellington's would be appropriate, someone distant enough to be difficult to locate in Debrett's. Direct funds to run Longleat Manor indefinitely.

Camille swallowed hard and sat back on her heels. Scrambled to her feet to pilfer through the correspondence scattered across the desk. A completed letter was there, addressed to the Tierney family's solicitor in London. Apparently, Tristan's solution to the problem, *her* problem, had been to create an inheritance. So she needn't marry Ridley.

Or him.

The air quite literally vanished from her lungs.

Hand trembling, she grabbed a quill pen, dipped the tip in the inkwell, and scribbled her opinion across the top of the letter.

Then she dressed and stalked from Tierney Hall's hunting lodge.

And took her blasted plums with her.

~

Tristan roused slowly, groggy after what felt like hours of actual sleep. He could only think, *I've found my duchess.* Under his nose all along. This, followed by a private declaration that should have scared the piss from him but didn't, *I'm getting married.*

Maybe even before Christmas.

He turned, smoothing his hand over her side of the bed. Sunlight was edging in around the drawn curtains, a pleasing frame of gold. Daylight. A full night's sleep, the first in years. Stretching, he smiled to himself. Her side of the bed. He liked the sound of that. Camille would always have a side with him from now on. She was the answer to his dreams. His path to the future, to happiness, to peace. To think, he'd considered letting Ridley marry her. Even if she hadn't cried off, even if they hadn't sealed their fate during a lush, remarkable night, *that* wouldn't have happened.

A daft idiot, he'd been twitching with jealousy since the night of his return.

He sat up, a slight twinge pinging his back, guessing

Camille was rounding up food as they'd eaten nothing last night. They'd swigged wine and whispered and laughed and made love. Again. And again. The last time shoved against the wall, him holding her up, hence the pain in his back. She had this neat trick, sucking on his tongue when she kissed him, which made him lose his mind. Lose. His. Mind. And her eyes, they'd gone this exacting shade of green, like fresh limes, when she slid over the brink. Impossibly beautiful.

And horribly arousing.

He'd never experienced a night like it, a woman like it, not once, not ever. He'd known he would marry her, so he'd remained inside her to completion, the first time he'd ever done that. *Bliss.*

His cock boosted the sheet as images commandeered his mind. Camille astride him, underneath him, legs locked around his waist, arms looped around his neck. Her mind invading his. She'd asked curious, delightful questions about other positions, other locations.

Was it possible on a chair? Outside? In the bath?

She'd damn-near talked him into a state of frenzy.

With the winter sunlight flowing over him, his body spent, his heart light, he accepted his existence was shifting. He was going to make Camille his duchess, then have a family. Have a life. Build her the finest greenhouse in England. Repair his tenant's homes and the village's roads, build a new school, and expand the church. He had ideas, thousands of them. He'd simply needed someone to help bring them into play.

He'd needed a reason to live again.

He'd found one. Found her.

The lengthening silence and extreme chill in the room began to register. The crack of a branch against the windowpane, wind whistling down an empty hearth, but nothing from inside the lodge. Not a breath aside from his. He drew one scented with her tantalizing essence as a flash of unease stirred his senses.

His gaze landed on his desk, papers jumbled, the letters he'd started then balled up in frustration and chucked to the floor tossed about. His effort to find a way out of having Camille marry Ridley without Tristan having to marry her himself. Scrambling from the bed, he approached the mess as if it were a blazing coal someone had asked him to shove down his trousers. Hesitant but certain, his belly clenched, a gut-sure feeling he usually paid attention to.

Oh, no. Not good.

Her handwriting, exhibited in a hastily-sketched note across the top of the letter, was lovely and delicate and strong. As she was.

Fury pulsed from her words like blood from a wound.

You have honor, I have pride. Thank you, but no.

"Bloody hell," Tristan whispered and crushed the vellum in his fist.

He stalked into the main room of the lodge, searching the corner where she'd dropped them yesterday. No basket, no plums.

Bracing his hand on the wall, he hung his head with a stricken groan.

A *very* angry future duchess was on the loose. And a *very* persistent duke was going to catch her.

~

"Where is she?" Tristan snapped as he stalked into Lady Fontaine's lavender parlor two hours later. Her favorite room, and the one she'd summoned him to for every gentle scolding of his youth, it fairly pulsed with femininity and stylish restraint. And the raw scent of pine. She stood before that silly tree he'd chopped down a mere four days ago, when it seemed like a hundred, her smile coy, sly, curling wickedly at the edges.

Oh, he just *bet* she loved this.

"My darling duke. What a surprise." She turned a sparkly silver ball in her hand and hung it from a branch. Tapped it once to send it swinging. "Or not."

He took a fast step forward, into the room. "Consider me foolish, but I have a feeling Camille isn't here. That she's gone racing off in a fit of ire you made no effort to talk her out of." He yanked his beaver hat from his head and muscled his fingers through his hair. "Am I correct?"

Lady Fontaine held up a slim tallow candle. "Not a good idea to place these on the tree, do you agree? Lady Markem tried tapers on hers. Gorgeous, those sparks of light. Until the wood caught fire. Torched her parlor *and* the library." She sighed and set the candle atop the hearth mantle. "Lord Markem is most displeased."

"You could have stopped her." He slapped his hat against his thigh, then jammed it back on his head, entirely willing to be impolite in the presence of a lady. He'd dressed for London, known he was likely heading there. Oswald was in the carriage, stewing, annoyed to be running back to Town before his promised holiday was complete. Now, he had a furious woman and valet to soothe. "You've been dangling your niece before me like a tasty biscuit since I arrived in Yorkshire, and now that I've taken a bite, you let her leave?"

"Certainly, I could have kept her here." She hung a length of crimson yarn and stepped back to review her display. "But where's the fun in making things too easy, darling?"

"I'm going to make her my duchess, so there's nothing scandalous about my intentions, should you be wondering. There was no need to introduce competition into the proceedings when there's always been too much."

"Oh, you foolish boy, I know that. I know *you*. Tristan

Tierney, honorable to his bones. I never expected less." She closed the distance between them and tilted his head from his study of the Aubusson rug—until he had nowhere to look but into her wise, knowing gaze. "At least she didn't want to leave."

Tristan perked up at this. "She didn't?"

Lady Fontaine patted his cheek. "You must have been impressive, aside from your rather amateurish wooing. I had to practically push her out the door while she was listing the many reasons to flee."

"*Where*, Bel?"

"She decided to spend the holiday with Edward if you must know. In that filthy city. Leaving me to water the plants in the conservatory on a dreadfully regimented schedule. I'll be running out there three times a day, thanks to your abysmal courting skills."

"I have no idea how to court anyone. I've never *been* in love before."

Lady Fontaine's eyes pooled with tears. Sniffing, she leaned in to hug him. He hugged her back, the woman who'd been more of a mother to him than his own. "Chase your duchess, my darling. Prove to her you will."

So chase he would.

CHAPTER 7

Where a future duchess receives an invitation.

Tristan stepped through the doorway of White's two days later and into a world he'd left behind. Before the war, he'd been a part of this, he recalled as he gazed around the candlelit room, holly and mistletoe hung here and there to provide a whiff of the season. Murmured conversation over brandy and gin, knowing laughter, ribald jokes, cards, dice, a fresh copy of *The Times* on every table.

The solid fragrance of wealth and promise, and at times, despair.

He gave his coat, hat, and cane to an attendant and moved to the salon he'd been directed to, the last on the left. Not a private room; Edward Bellington, the Marquess of Rutherford, couldn't afford private lodgings, not if his ancestral estate was in financial distress. Tristan suspected he was even having trouble paying his dues, but some things in society were compulsory.

Or seemed it.

Tristan shook off the dispiriting thought and crossed into the dimly-lit salon. His childhood friend sat in a tufted armchair, book in hand, tumbler by his side, firelight rolling over him in tawny waves. He had Camille's nose, or she his. The shape of the eyes the same but not the coloring. The hair, no, not quite. Camille's was thicker, lush, silky, as you desired when you were tunneling your hands through it.

"Are you coming in, Tris, or are you going to stand there deliberating about the wallpaper?"

Tristan pushed off his doorjamb perch and strolled inside, his heart seizing at what he needed to say, the speech he'd practiced on the carriage ride over. Camille's father was deceased, so this left Edward as head of the Bellington family. It was this man, his closest friend, he'd have to open his heart to.

I'm in love with your sister. The one who battled the angry swan, the termagant. Yes, that's her.

Instead, he held his composure, pouring brandy from the decanter on the sideboard, then crossing to sprawl in the seat opposite Edward. Kicking one polished Hessian atop the other, he released a modest yawn. "How is she?" he asked, charging in right off, ruining his strategy to discuss London's foul weather before diving into the *real* reason he was in town.

To chase down the man's hellion of a sister.

Edward dipped his head, his laughter so familiar, so welcome, Tristan's gut clenched. Affection poured over him like a drenching rain, washing away any fear he'd had that they'd misplaced their friendship.

"I'm not sure what you find so amusing," Tristan mumbled into his glass.

Edward propped his chin on his fist and grinned. It was Camille's maddening smile, to be sure, slapped across her brother's handsome face. "I'm sure you don't. The ones stuck in it never do. I'm going to wring every ounce of joy from this. London is boring as hell during the winter, don't you know? This, you and Camille, is more than I'd hoped for, more than I'd dreamed of. God knows, she worked for it, the tenacious sprite, hanging in there until the end. Imagine, the two people, aside from my wife, I love most in the world finding each other. Unbelievable." He sipped slowly, his smile positively luminous. "I wondered how long it'd be before you arrived. Less than three days, I said to myself, means the man is besotted. And you made it in *two*. That's blind love, which Camille deserves, of course, referring back to all the work she put into getting you. Although she's a challenge, shall we say, a bit fractious. Likes to get her way." He raised his glass in a toast. "Good luck to you, my dearest friend. You have my blessing and my sympathy in advance for the nights you get booted from your home by your loving duchess and are forced to sleep on my settee."

Well, Tristan reasoned, with relief and a surge of irritation. "I sprinted to town like a feral dog, worried about what she might do, owing to that"—he grimaced—"*fractious* nature. I already know what I'm getting, and no matter the complexity, I want it. I want *her*. And if *you* want Ridley to continue breathing, you'd better make damn sure he doesn't put one polished patent pump in my way."

"I'd never have stood by while she married Ridley, Tris. I'd only heard about the arrangement myself. The chit made an impulsive decision, the bills at Longleat piling up even worse than I'd imagined. My fault completely. Love took my eye off the ball, my race to the altar being about as tricky as yours is proving to be. I would have found a way to prop the estate up. I *will*. I'm not expecting you to step in."

"Longleat is as much my home as hers, in my heart anyway. I want to save it. You can't help what your father did. His gambling ruined the family. You were a boy, nothing you could have done to stop him." He cut a sharp glance from the corner of his eye. "However, I'm not the only prideful one, although Camille tops me by miles. I don't want her to marry me for the Mercer fortune, which is substantial, I admit. Even if she turns me down, you and I will figure this out. My solicitors are researching a new business venture, which will mean going into trade, a blasphemy to the *ton*, I know. You'd be cut because of it, marquess or no, but you'll never have to worry about blunt again." Coughing lightly to cover his discomfiture, Tristan shrugged. "We're partners is what I'm trying to say, even if Camille breaks my bloody heart."

Edward peeled out of his slouch, brandy flecking his crisp, white cuff. "You haven't asked her yet? Oh, this is a fine fiddle. I assumed a graceless proposal was the problem."

Tristan released an affronted snort. "Not to divulge too much about private matters, but she ran away before I could."

Edward's mouth opened, advice Tristan didn't want to hear set to tumble out when they were fortuitously interrupted.

"Rutherford, about your sister—" The man, a corpulent baron who imagined himself an academic, stumbled to a halt in the doorway. Tristan had met him on two occasions and had come away from both unimpressed. "Sorry, sorry, didn't know you were entertaining. Evening, Your Grace."

Tristan tipped his head in acknowledgment. "Quigley."

The baron shifted from one foot to the other. Tristan had been told he had an unnerving way of staring at people, which he often used to his advantage. "Let me leave you two to your talk. I'll send a note around, arrange a time. What say you, Rutherford?"

Tristan shot an exploratory glance at Edward, catching his startled expression, the fingers tapping a jumpy rhythm on his knee, and decided to play the game. After all, his friend had wanted a spot of fun, hadn't he? "Oh, my no, Quigley. I'm a family acquaintance of long-standing. You can speak in front of me." Rising to his feet, Tristan strode to the sideboard, poured a liberal measure, and offered it to the baron. No one in society would turn down a drink from a duke.

Not when the duke rarely offered.

"Now that you ask, I think I will sink in for a little chinwag," Quigley said and dragged a threadbare chair Tristan hoped would hold him into their circle.

Tristan reclaimed his seat and gestured to Quigley. "You were saying, about Lady Bellington..." Out of the corner of his eye, he watched Edward deflate like a balloon pricked by a barb, sliding low in his chair as he drained his glass.

"I can't allow her to speak at the botanical society meeting, Rutherford, I simply can't. You understand I'm sure." Quigley misinterpreted Edward's groan as directed at him when it was likely meant to describe the general situation the marquess found himself in. "She's been writing to us for two years as this C.E. Bellington fellow. Lots of marvelous information on ways to fertilize azaleas and calm acute oak decline. This latest variety of plum is news the entire botanical world must hear. But, and this is the kicker, who'd imagine an intelligent bloke like that to be...to be a *woman?*"

Tristan sipped slowly, the fury that had frequently bitten him on the battlefield nipping at the base of his spine. "A female botanist. Quite remarkable, isn't it?"

"Absurd is what it is," Quigley said around a smacking swallow.

Edward whispered an oath and hung his hands between his legs, staring at them rather than joining the conversation.

Tristan let the mantel clock tick off ten seconds before

speaking. "I think it's fascinating. Charming. Courageous. Like the lady."

Quigley paused, the tense undercurrent in the room finally piercing his awareness. "What's it to you, Mercer?"

"Ah, well"—Tristan balanced his glass on his belly and steepled his fingers atop the crystal—"it means quite a lot to me actually. The world, as it were."

Quigley's blotchy cheeks expanded with his breath. "Fancy bluestockings? No idea. Thought you were into actresses."

Tristan clenched his jaw and listened to the clock tick, half a minute this time. "I'm a benefactor of the National History Museum, Quigley, did you know? The events we've attended there over the years ring a bell? Your society, my funds. Botanical prints are rather expensive, as I recall. When most in the *ton* aren't able to afford the expense. To put it tastelessly, I would hate for your group to lose the opportunity to acquire them."

Quigley blustered and rocked forward in his chair. It squeaked and swayed but held steady. "The botanical illustration collection? But we've found a new print by an artist in Wales that is easily the best rendition of an ophrys apifera you've ever seen."

"I do not doubt as I've seen none." Tristan pulled a thread from his sleeve and flicked it to the floor. "Is this spectacular Welsh artist willing to donate his work, by any chance?"

Quigley swallowed, his jaw clenching as he started to get the picture. "Well, in fact, no."

"Excellent! A fine businessman your artiste in addition to being a creative genius. We're agreed then." Tristan sat up and held out his hand to seal the deal, an American tradition he planned to start regularly employing because his countrymen disliked it so much.

Quigley set his glass on the table with a click but kept his hand in his lap like Tristan had threatened to sever it at the wrist. "Agreed to *what* exactly?"

"You let C. E. Bellington speak at your esteemed society meetings any time she feels the need, and I continue to underwrite paintings of carrot roots and sunflowers and the like." Tristan experienced the strangest surge of happiness as the next words rolled from his lips, proving he was, indeed, desperately in love. "Your venerated society certainly wouldn't take part in rebuffing a duchess. *My* duchess."

"She's going to kill you," Edward muttered behind the fist he dragged across his mouth.

Quigley collapsed in his chair, astonishment evident in face and form. "What is England coming to when a duke chooses an intellectual? A woman who reads actual *books*. Not novels, mind you, but science texts. And writes articles fit for an Oxford professor. Society is crumbling, frankly decaying around us. They're going to take over. This is what you're setting in motion, Mercer. Women ruling the world." He reclaimed his glass and knocked it back, a crimson drop running down his chin and bleeding into his crumpled collar. "My God, her needlework is probably horrific. You'll have no uplifting quoted cushions scattered about, that's my verdict."

Tristan looked to Edward, who shook his head sadly.

"Cheer up, Quigley. She can't sew a stitch, play the pianoforte or paint adequate landscapes, true." Tristan's smile was swift and sharp. "But those plums are the bloody best you've ever tasted in your life."

CHAPTER 8

Where a besotted duke gets an earful.

Camille shifted the note she'd received an hour prior into the murky light cast from Edward's carriage lamp and read it for the hundredth time.

...the society would be delighted to discuss the new species of plum tree...please contact us to arrange a time at your earliest convenience...

And the closing line, one seizing her insides until she struggled for lucidity.

Congratulations on your engagement to the Duke of Mercer.

Camille forced the air trapped in her lungs into the frigid London evening and rapped on the trap to tell the coachman to pick up the pace.

Murder would not be good enough when she got her hands on him.

And once she was done with Tristan, she was going after

her brother. He'd commented, very subtly over kippers and toast, about running into Tristan at White's.

Oh, both the men she loved were going to pay.

The streets were a catastrophe, filled with hordes preparing for a holiday a mere five days away. The scent of cinnamon and gingerbread wafting from the shops drifted through a crack in the carriage's window, overriding the stink of burning coal and river blight, a careless delight Camille would have otherwise taken great pleasure in. As it was, keeping the furious crimson haze from spilling out of her soul and staining the city's cobblestones was taking every fiber of her being.

She scrambled from the carriage when it halted before Tierney House, ignoring the coachman's offer of assistance, splattering the hem of her gown and ruining her slippers as she landed in an icy puddle. She cursed and took the front stairs like a madwoman, snow coloring the night in a wistful, white mist. Then she did something she'd never done or considered doing and rushed into a private residence without knocking.

Tristan's majordomo caught her before she'd made it three steps, his startled gasp echoing off the exquisite walnut lining the vestibule. "Not another one," he huffed and reached for her arm, the ring of keys in his hand jangling.

Camille pulled to a stop, wrenching out of his hold. "Another one?" she said in horror. Oh, *oh*, Tristan Fitzhugh Tierney was a *dead* duke. "Where is he?"

"Madam, please, I realize as an actress you must emote but calm yourself." He smoothed his hand down a severely tailored lapel and pulled himself to his full height, which brought him eye-level with Camille. "My name is Brixworth, and whatever Your Grace has done, we can correct. If you'll only retire to the parlor to your right, I'll bring—"

"I'm not giving your employer one additional ducal *second*

to prepare for this meeting, Brixworth," Camille returned and marched down the hallway. Paintings of the Tierney ancestors lined the walls, aristocratic disdain shadowing her step as the scent of woodsmoke and sandalwood guided her.

The study door was open. A cozy space bathed in amber housing floor-to-ceiling bookcases and exceptional works of art. And Tristan. Sprawled in a leather armchair perfectly suited to his long, lean body, a stack of letters and a glass on the table beside him, his legs crossed at the ankle and going on for miles. He appeared every inch a formidable aristocrat at his leisure, clothing rumpled but first-rate, hair mussed, jaw shadowed just enough to make him look dangerous.

His gaze lifted to hers and the flash of absolute joy on his face pierced her like a splinter.

Stomping forward, she balled up the botanical society's letter and tossed the crumpled parchment in his face. "The botanical society is congratulating me on my engagement!"

He didn't pretend to miss her meaning, a lazy smile drifting across his face. His emerald eyes glowed as he stared up at her, damn him. "You saved me a trip to Edward's. How fortuitous."

"You arrogant boor, you controlling beast!"

"Damn, did I miss you," Tristan said, and before she could blink, yanked her into his lap. For one weak instant, she sank into his hard body, then she stiffened and wrenched back.

"Your Grace," Brixworth sputtered in dismay from the doorway. "I warned you about the dramatic ones. Much cannot be left on the stage."

"Let me up," Camille breathed, struggling to gain her footing, "and I'll show him dramatic."

Sliding his hand around her neck, Tristan closed the scant distance between them, pressing his lips to hers as Brixworth coughed and shuffled behind them. A gentle touch but one with enough persuasion to bring her thrashing to an abrupt halt. "I love you," he whispered for her alone. "I would have told you, bathed you in adoration, if you hadn't run away from me after what was the most magical night of my life."

Abruptly, and uncharacteristically, Camille dropped her face to his shoulder and burst into tears. She hadn't slept more than two hours in days, and this muddle was the last straw. His body shifted beneath her as he waved Brixworth away, the door closing behind the majordomo. With a sigh, Tristan gave up any pretense of propriety and pulled her against his broad chest.

"What is this," he murmured into her hair. "Botanists don't cry. Upsets the plants, don't you know."

She sniffled. "Well, apparently actresses do. Your…"—she swallowed back a sob and dug her cheek into his fine woolen coat—"favorite."

He exhaled, the sound pained. "There was one, long ago, as you and the rest of England know. Before the war, before I knew what I wanted, what I needed. It's so trite a comment to make, and a typically masculine one, I realize, but it meant nothing, means nothing." His arms tensed around her, his passionate speech stealing in and nicking her ire. "There isn't anyone else in my mind or my heart. You're the only woman, no matter what you decide, I will *ever* ask to be my duchess. I swear this to you. C.E. Bellington, botanist and swan tormentor, you are my life. I want you, every part of you. I want a family, a future. I think I always have. I just had to find the courage to admit it."

She lifted her head, her watery gaze finding his. "You forced the society's hand. When maybe I needed to do this on my own. When I *wanted* to do it on my own." Bracing her arm on his chest, his scattered heartbeat flowed through her fingertips and up her arm. "How can I stay mad at you when you say all these lovely things and you know I've loved you forever? Wanted you even longer."

His smile was bashful, and he ducked his head with a short, sharp shrug to hide it. "I did force their hand, the imbeciles. I'm a scoundrel, but it felt wonderful. Isn't this damned title worth anything? Am I not allowed to barter it to buy what I want from time to time? Consider it my ham-fisted wedding present to you. A thousand future discussions with the oh-so-tedious botanical society delegate. They'll love you because decision-making over where our funds go now rests in your capable hands. Quigley won't argue, not when he wants a new drawing of some bloody plant."

She closed her eyes, unable to look in the face of the man she'd cherished her entire life and reasonably puzzle this out. He was placing societal power, power she'd never considered having, in her lap.

"You could be pregnant," he whispered after a charged silence.

"So that's it," she said with a sinking heart, another round of tears stinging the back of her eyes. Perhaps she was, although it was too soon to know. She'd been overly emotional since their night of lovemaking. Probably just what love did to twist one's sanity in a knot.

"No, that's *not* it." Tristan cursed and gave her a shake. "I love you. *That's* it. Isn't love more than enough? I'm sorry you can't have what you deserve, Princess. Respect for your intelligence, the highest regard for your knowledge, a place in the botanical world you are given because you've earned it, because you're gifted. Society doesn't, as yet, allow this for women. You'll have to settle for the love of a man who can move mountains, willingly, for you." He whisked his thumb over her cheek, her lips, following the caress with his mouth. "Invite me into your life, because I so want to be there."

The kiss was molten, rich, permeating to her bones. His hand traveled a now-familiar path, awakening each part of her body he touched. The sound of ice pinging the windowpane and the crackle of the hearthfire receded until they were alone, the world no bigger than this small space in a Mayfair townhouse. His body reacted, his sex lengthening beneath her bottom. Unable to arrest the impulse, she wriggled against him with a ragged sigh.

"Maybe you don't *need* me," he breathed against her lips, " but maybe you want me. Even if you shouldn't. Let's start there, because I want you. Which I definitely should."

Camille dropped her brow to his and felt love tear down the walls she'd placed around her heart.

For one rushed second, before the deal was done, she imagined a future without Tristan. The decision—*yes*—was simple when she registered the dreadful feeling engulfing her.

She *couldn't* live without him.

"You can keep yourself and have me, too. I'm not asking you to fade into me and lose what makes you *you*." Tristan trailed his finger down her cheek, her jaw, and into the neckline of her bodice. Her nipples strained, begging for release. He wasn't fighting fairly, but then again, she didn't want him to. "No more chasing a duke is required. Unless you'd like to catch him."

Camille smiled and seized his lips beneath hers, deciding that was a promise she meant to make her devilish duke keep.

EPILOGUE

Where a duke and duchess get a happy ending.

Tierney Hall, North Yorkshire
Three years later

Camille tiptoed into the darkened bedchamber, her breath suspended. The room was bathed in milky light and was, remarkably, divinely silent. Dusting potting soil from her fingertips, she approached the bed, and her heart, as it often did, dropped to her knees.

The duke and his heir were fast asleep. Lying on their sides facing each other, chests rising and falling in an exhausted tempo. Tristan's arm was secured solidly around their son's tiny waist to keep him from rolling off the bed. They'd managed to wear each other out if the books and toys scattered across the space were any indication.

She perched on the edge of the mattress and brushed a lock of hair the exact color of Tristan's, right down to the amber tips, from her son's cheek. Except for the nose he'd inherited from her, and possibly his stubborn little chin, he looked exactly, astoundingly, like his father.

Oh, Tris, she thought in gratitude and love.

She'd not known a man could be such a carefree father, could cherish a child with such intensity. When they'd found out she was pregnant a month after their wedding, she hadn't expected Tristan to be so engaged. So elated. In the *ton*, it simply wasn't done. Her father had barely paid attention to her or her brother—and he'd never seemed *happy* about having children. Yet, Tristan was so involved she'd found time to research a stouter species of English rose, record data on the growth of her Sussex plum and consult on the construction of a new conservatory at Tierney Hall. They had help, obviously, a large staff, but Tristan preferred to do much with and for Ethan himself.

"For God's sake, don't wake him up," her husband muttered from the depths of his pillow. "Unless you want to see a duke cry."

Camille laughed, very softly, and started to rub Tristan's back, the gentle circles he liked best. "How can a tiny boy cause such strife? You must be mistaken. Ethan is an angel."

He hummed lazily beneath his breath, on the verge of dropping back to sleep. "I chased him around this chamber until I grew faint and had to sit down. Embarrassing to be outmanned by a two-year-old."

Camille stretched out behind Tristan, throwing an arm over his hips and fitting her body to his. His skin was hot, his body hard. A faint quiver moved through her limbs and settled between her thighs. "You're so good with him, Tris."

The mattress dipped as he tugged the sheet to Ethan's chest. "I don't know how. I love him so much I guess it comes naturally. Like it does with you. With everyone else, I'm rubbish."

"Natural makes me think of certain activities, activities best performed without clothing." She nibbled on a sensitive patch below his ear, and he groaned with delight. Her hand trailed beneath the counterpane, down his chest, over his flat belly, and into his waistband. He was hard and pulsing, ready for her. "Do you want to seize this opportunity and sneak off to my bedchamber? I don't sleep there, so we should use the room for something."

Tristan lifted his head, glanced over his shoulder. His eyes were turning a spectacular, mossy green, meaning he was about to kiss every thought from her mind. "I think I can summon the strength, since you're asking so nicely, being an agreeable husband and all." His lips lifted in the lazy smile that had her insides melting and doing a dreamy slide to the floor. "You know what your blistering look does to me, Princess." Without disturbing their son, Tristan rolled over and sank his hand into her hair and pulled her into another world, his world, *their* world. "How long will it take to summon the nursemaid?"

Ethan's wispy snore ripped them apart. Camille rolled from the bed, held up a hand that shook. After all this time, her husband still made her tremble. "I'll meet you in my bedchamber. Five minutes." She crossed the chamber, then turned to find him sitting up in bed, his expression joyful, his gaze scorching. "No, make it four."

"Princess," he called as she opened the door.

She looked back.

"I love you. You two"—he nodded to Ethan—"are my life."

Her heart fluttered, her pulse kicked. "Three minutes," she amended and gave him a luminous smile. "And I'll gladly give chase if I have to."

THE END

Thank you for reading *Chasing the Duke*! You may have noticed I took minor liberties with the story. I wanted Tristan to have the opportunity to chop down a Christmas tree for Camille, so I moved this tradition's start date up a few years. It actually began in England in 1848, when Queen Victoria's husband, Prince Albert, placed one in Windsor Castle. It was originally a German tradition, as I stated in *Chasing*. Also, the plum tree Camille is so proud of is real—it's called a Victoria plum and was discovered by a Sussex nurseryman in 1840.

Stick around for an excerpt of the next installment of the **12 Days of Christmas Series**: Mayfair Maiden by Annabelle Anders.

CHAPTER ONE

Peter Spencer, third son of the Earl of Ravensdale, leaned forward in his chair and slid his left hand downward, his fingers ghosting over the strings as his thumb caressed the smooth wood that made up the neck of the cello.

Without question, he felt more comfortable with the curved instrument resting snugly between his legs than he felt doing almost anything else. He didn't require an audience. He didn't require praise. And yet…

Blood thrummed through his veins, knowing that in less than one week, he would be studying under the finest cellist in all of England. HIs gaze skimming the perimeter of the gilded ballroom, he smiled to himself. He would not miss London society over the next six months. He'd never truly fit in with the other gents, playing cards, wagering and pursuing other gentlemanly and not so gentlemanly entertainments. He'd always sensed that he belonged somewhere else.

Only a few lingering guests remained in the massive room, most having moved into the adjacent hall where supper was being served. There would be dancing after, but he'd fulfilled his obligation as guest musician for the night,

CHAPTER ONE

leaving him free to bow out for the remainder of the evening. If left to him, he would decline these invitations altogether. His mother, however, had a most annoying habit of accepting them on his behalf.

He plucked a soft arpeggio, contemplating the farewell party his brother had threatened. Stone had mentioned scotch, cards, and a brothel—not necessarily in that order.

For God's sake, it wasn't as though Peter was getting married. He was simply moving to Brighton. The shine of Golden-red flashed across the room. Not fire, but it might as well be.

The widowed Countess Starling. She stood nearby, partially hidden by a large column, staring out the terrace windows, hugging her arms in front of herself.

This lady was living proof that beauty and wealth didn't always equal happiness. Earlier, from his vantage point in the dais, he'd observed a cluster of popular ladies blatantly give her the cut direct. She'd handled it well, lifting her chin and moving along, not missing a step.

But he'd seen it. The hurt, the almost imperceptible shudder of pain. And now, rather than follow the crowd into the supper room, she held herself back.

She turned and met his gaze. Forest-green eyes, alabaster skin, and an hourglass figure to rival all figures.

He rose. "My Lady," he acknowledged her, balancing Rosa on her endpin. Since the first time he'd met the widow last summer at one of his mother's house parties, she had intrigued him.

Not only because of her beauty. Numerous nubile young beauties paraded themselves in society and hardly any of them ever captured his attention beyond a fleeting appreciation.

No, Lady Starling intrigued him because of her failed

CHAPTER ONE

potential. She reminded him of a perfectly made violin that no one had ever bothered to tune.

Unfortunately, she also intimidated the hell out of him.

"Do you ever dance?" Her voice echoed in the empty hall.

Peter narrowed his eyes and pushed a wayward lock of hair out of his eyes. She didn't appear to be hinting that she was seeking him out as an escort.

"On occasion, but I prefer to be on this side of the dancefloor." He indicated the small box where the orchestra played.

Her posture tugged at him, evoking a myriad of conflicting emotions.

Pity. Desire. And something else. Something he couldn't quite put his finger on.

Peter ignored the urge to settle his gaze on her full bosoms, or round, inviting hips and dipped his chin to stare down at his instrument. A less volatile curvaceous lady—one who would never betray him, a lady who would give her best so long as he took care of her properly.

"I hate dancing." Her voice clipped, almost as though she was speaking to herself. "At least you have an excuse to avoid it."

He glanced back up in time to see her drag a disparaging gaze over his cello. He was oddly offended on behalf of his instrument.

"I thought you were staying with your husband's family in Brighton this spring." Although her absence hadn't kept her out of the latest scandal. The scandal, in fact, that led to Baron Chaswick's hasty society wedding.

"My in-laws try my patience. They were my husband's family, never mine. Nothing for me there." The droll tone of her voice hitched as she glanced toward the windows. "Perhaps nothing for me here, either."

CHAPTER ONE

Peter frowned, not so much at her circumstances, but at his response to the pain revealed when her façade slipped.

No doubt, Lord Starling's sisters had been less than welcoming. The Earl of Starling had been thirty years his wife's senior. His family would not have accepted this his widow warmly, as was usually the case when a wealthy and titled gentleman married a much younger beautiful woman.

From what he'd heard of her sexual prowess, however, he could assume she'd kept the old man happy in his last days. His cohort, Chaswick, had attested to that after having embarked on an affair with her at a house party earlier that year.

"I've finished playing for the night," he surprised himself by saying. "Will you join me at a table in the supper room?" He wasn't hungry. He'd intended to pack Rosa up and send for his carriage.

She shrugged, forcing a half-smile. A flame-colored curl fell forward, drawing Peter's attention to her expansive décolletage. "Yes. Perhaps. No."

Her ambiguous response reminded him why he'd never approached her before. It wasn't polite to sit when a lady remained standing in his presence, but the usual rules didn't apply here, did they?

He lowered himself, thinking to experiment with a particular run that had been playing through his mind. He pressed his fingers onto the strings, sliding them down, a motion that felt as familiar to him as walking.

And then she sighed.

A melodic sigh that slid from a high 'D' to low 'D', spanning a perfect octave. It sent a warmth down his spine and had him staring at her again, noticing the curve of her neck, feminine and fragile. And the delicate slope of her shoulders.

"A stroll through the gardens then?" Likely, she'd refuse him again.

CHAPTER ONE

He rubbed a hand beneath his cravat and then rolled his shoulders. Damned hot in here. Halfway through the Season, one couldn't escape the heat in even the most spectacular of Mayfair ballrooms. Especially after it had accommodated a few hundred sweating, dancing humans for several hours. Add to that the flames from all the candles...

He'd need to pack Rosa up first.

Lady Starling sent him a suspicious sideways glance. "Wouldn't you prefer to ask one of the debutantes? I'm not fooled by your musical obsession, Mister Spencer. You're one of Ravensdale's sons, and sought after as much as any titled gentleman."

Peter could only laugh at that. He was the third son of an earl—granted, an incredibly wealthy earl, ensuring that he would never lack funds. But his estate, Millcot Lodge in Essex, was a modest one, and he would never hold a title.

Which was perfectly fine with him as he was rather fond of his father and two older brothers—even if Stone had the most annoying habit of bruising his arm with the occasional brotherly sock.

"I'm not interested in escorting a Mayfair maiden. I'm interested in walking you." Because she had no marriage-minded mama who'd be watching his every move with her daughter. It wouldn't be significant for him to be spotted alone with a widow.

But more than that. He was *interested* in her. He had been for some time now.

"Very well." It wasn't a resoundingly enthusiastic response, but he doubted the lady was ever resoundingly enthusiastic for much of anything.

"Allow me a moment to put Rosa away." Carefully setting his cello to the side, he opened the large leather case that had been custom built to protect her for transport.

"You named it?" The question, like everything else she

had said to this point, came out in mocking tones. Knowing it was a part of her armor, it didn't bother him.

"She," Peter corrected her. "She's more than a possession. She's my life. The least she deserves is a name, don't you think?"

Lady Starling's throat moved, as though his answer was difficult to swallow. "But it, pardon me, *she*, is replaceable. She's an inanimate object—wood, metal, glue."

Peter snapped the metal closures into place and stroked a hand along the leather. "But for now, she owns my heart." It was the only way he could explain how he felt about the instrument. He'd owned several others before Rosa and cared equally for each and every one of them. But for today, Rosa was the one that brought his music to life.

He moved around to the opening of the dais, vaguely aware that Lady Starling drifted in the same direction to meet him.

"Shall I send for your wrap?" The evening was warm, but her gown might leave her catching a chill. By no means current on ladies' fashion, Peter would nonetheless wager a year's allowance that the plunging bodice of her garment challenged societal boundaries. The brilliant forest-green silk, almost identical to the color of her eyes, cinched in at her waist. The off-the-shoulder puffed sleeves draped lazily into the crooks of her elbows, where long satin gloves ended.

"I'm fine." Her answer belied her expression. She was far from fine.

Peter winged an arm. "Shall we, then?"

ABOUT TRACY SUMNER

Tracy's story telling career began when she picked up a copy of LaVyrle Spencer's Vows on a college beach trip. A journalism degree and a thousand romance novels later, she decided to try her hand at writing a southern version of the perfect love story. With a great deal of luck and more than a bit of perseverance, she sold her first novel to Kensington Publishing.

When not writing sensual stories featuring complex characters and lush settings, Tracy can be found reading romance, snowboarding, watching college football and figuring out how she can get to 100 countries before she kicks. She lives in the south, but after spending a few years in NYC, considers herself a New Yorker at heart.

Tracy has been awarded the National Reader's Choice, the Write Touch and the Beacon—with finalist nominations in the HOLT Medallion, Heart of Romance, Rising Stars and Reader's Choice. Her books have been translated into German, Dutch, Portuguese and Spanish. She loves hearing from readers about why she tends to pit her hero and heroine against each other from the very first page or that great romance she simply must order in five seconds on her Kindle.

Connect with Tracy:

www.tracy-sumner.com

- facebook.com/Tracysumnerauthor
- twitter.com/sumnertrac
- instagram.com/tracysumnerromance
- bookbub.com/profile/tracy-sumner
- pinterest.com/tracysumnerromance

Made in United States
Troutdale, OR
10/25/2024